S
F
BOOKS

Planet Scumm is a triannual short fiction anthology. Visit **planetscumm.space** for submissions.

First Printing, 2022   ISBN: 978-1-970154-12-2

© SPARK & FIZZ BOOKS
Portland | Boston | Europa

SPARK & FIZZ BOOKS PRESENTS

PLANET SCUMM

SPRING 2022 — "SOMETHING UP AHEAD" — ISSUE NO. 13

— AN INTERDIMENSIONAL TABLE OF CONTENTS —

EDITOR-IN-CHIEF	CREATIVE DIRECTOR	MANAGING EDITOR	MARKETING DIRECTOR	IN-HOUSE DESIGNER
SEAN CLANCY	ALYSSA ALARCÓN SANTO	TYLER BERD	SAM RHEAUME	MAURA McGONAGLE

COVER AND SPOT ILLUSTRATIONS BY MAURA McGONAGLE
@MCMCGONAGLE

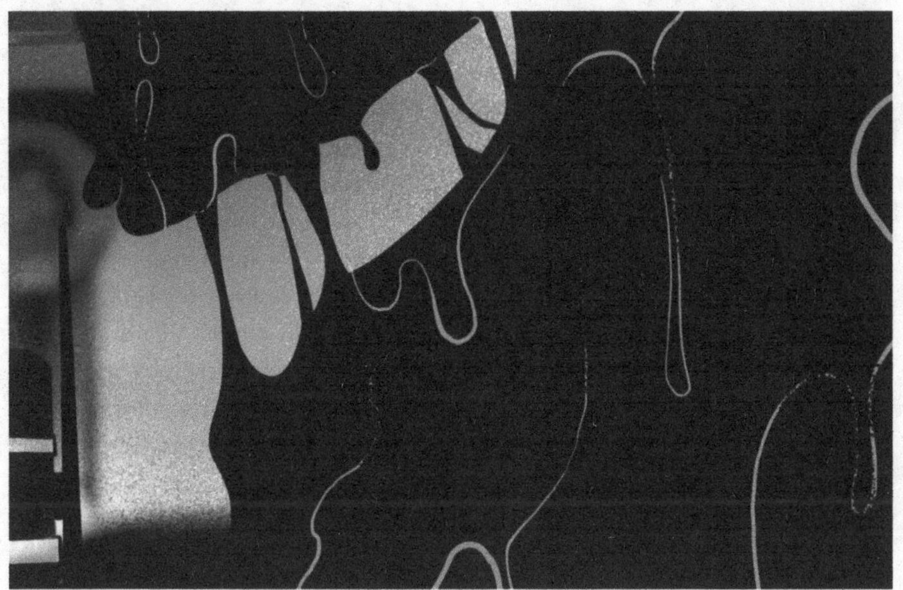

THE SCUMMY SPACE

You open a door and find yourself in a room. Empty and completely featureless, painted an alabaster white that seems to insist upon itself. Don't panic. Don't try to run. In fact, don't even make a noise, because soon our guests will be arriving—you can hear them moving behind the walls.

In a few moments this room will be quite busy indeed, populated by tales of the frightening and fantastic. They're comfortable here, because the bounds of this space aren't defined by mundane concrete or drywall.

No, the limits of this room are set only by the mind. Its ceiling rises to the height of humanity's ambition. Its foundation rests—uneasily, I might add—on our planet's collective fears. And in between... *the Scummy Space.*

Now, imagine if you will: a cave.

A stony abscess carved out by time, and filled with the rank pus of regret. Watch on, and you'll see a young girl approach the cave, and in doing so take a rather unconventional trip through history. Not her own, but that of a woman very much like her. For you see, in Chelsea Muzar's *"Cave of the Lost Frog Woman,"* history is always waiting just inside the entrance. And on this particular day, history is hungry.

We turn now to the humble radio.

Diminished in recent decades, and yet still the gold standard for mass communication in the modern era. In Lindsay King-Miller's *"Radio Elsewhere"* we'll be introduced to a peculiar example of this noble technological lineage. A radio that's quite vital to a mother and child on an impromptu trip. But whatever you do, don't change that station. Because the voices you hear on the local Top 40 might not be trustworthy. In fact, they might not exist at all.

On the topic of entertainment: consider gardening.

A rewarding pastime that has occupied the people of Earth through prosperity and hardship, through peace and war. But in Eli Wilkinson's contribution to our program, the plants of the world finally come to collect their due. And when the bill is totaled, it may just be that the green thumbs of the world will be first in line to serve as *"Fertilizer."*

From the wilds of experimental horticulture, we divert to the modern office building.

Clean. Economical. Efficient. Some would even say *too* efficient. Because in Andrew Zozma's *"A Man, Running,"* the humdrum day-to-day of mid-level corporate living can be a potent energy indeed. If every day feels exactly like the one before, perhaps it is—exactly. And more chilling: perhaps someone wants to keep it that way.

Continued dispatches on the topic of living death.

The location? Anytown, Earth. The time? Ten minutes past the apocalypse. Travel on and Henry Sanders-Wright will introduce us to a man looking for redemption after a life spent in drudgery. And "life" is the operative word here. Because our ostensible hero in *"There's Nobody Left to Haunt"* has two problems. The first is that he's dead. The second is that his corpse isn't quite dead enough.

Let's try a change of pace.

The protagonist of A. Katherine Black's *"Recesses of Uriel"* certainly wants one. She's an animal handler, of sorts, for creatures not entirely like our own on a planet that's similarly dissimilar. Anyone who works closely with animals will inevitably develop affection towards them, but for this particular "silker" that affection goes beyond one of professional convenience. And, if left alone, it may go beyond the hazy line that separates body from mind.

Love can be a fickle thing like that.

Doubly so in our next segment, Hailey Piper's *"Pleasant Guests with Better Games."* The holidays are in full swing at the family home, and the second youngest of the family is bringing a guest back from college. The past always looms large over the festive season, past both recent and ancient. And for this particular gathering, with this particular guest, the near and distant past will be defendant and plaintiff, respectively. Because the family aren't

THE SCUMMY SPACE

just hosting a guest this holiday— they're playing an ancient, deadly game. Rule number one: be kind, or else.

Finally, we'd like to remind our readers that *"The Scummy Space"* is brought to you thanks to the help of our wonderful sponsors. I'd like to talk to about one such sponsor now: Unidentified Aerial Phenomena.

That's right, when I'm done manning the Scummy Space here on *Planet Scumm*, I like to cruise around in my UAP. Four out of five aviation experts agree—there's no beating the smooth acceleration and seemingly impossible turning radius of UAPs. Don't take my word for it—you can read about the latest on UAPs in Paul Spears' *"Bureaucracy of Weird."*

Until next time friends, remember: between light and shadow, between heat and cold, and between salty and sweet, lies... *the Scummy Space.*

"SOMETHING UP AHEAD"

SPARK & FIZZ BOOKS, 2022
Portland | Boston | Europa

AUTHOR BIOS

CHELSEA MUZAR holds her Master's Degree in Creative Writing from the University of Nebraska Omaha. Her work has been published in *Clarkesworld Magazine, The Novice Writer, Kansas City Voices,* and other publications. When she isn't writing, she's spending time with her husband and their poodle puppy, Oliver.

LINDSAY KING-MILLER is the author of *Ask a Queer Chick: A Guide to Sex, Love, and Life for Girls who Dig Girls* (Plume, 2016). Her fiction has appeared in the anthologies *The Fiends in the Furrows* (Nosetouch, 2018), *Tiny Nightmares* (Catapult, 2020), and numerous other publications. She lives in Denver, CO.

ELI WILKINSON is a science fiction and horror writer, working out of the rainy wastes of Vancouver, Canada, where he lives with his wife and a dog. His work has previously appeared in *Uncanny Magazine's* "Disabled People Destroy Science Fiction" issue.

ANDREW KOZMA's fiction has been published in *Escape Pod, Daily Science Fiction,* and *Analog.* His book of poems, *City of Regret* (Zone 3 Press, 2007), won the Zone 3 First Book Award, and his second poetry book, *Orphanotrophia,* was recently published by Cobalt Press.

HENRY SANDERS-WRIGHT is a Project Manager by day and a writer by early morning/evening and has had work previously published in *All World's Wayfarer.* In between making thrilling production timelines and sending edge-of-your-seat emails, Henry imagines (and eventually writes) characters, worlds and stories across all speculative genres. He hasn't quite found his place yet, but he thinks he likes it that way. The best place to find him is @TheIrregularH on Twitter and irregularhenry on Instagram.

A. KATHERINE BLACK, is an audiologist and a writer. She adores multicolored pens, stories featuring giant and/or friendly spiders, and nearly everything at 2 am. She lives in a very small town with her family, their cats, and her overworked coffee machines. Her short fiction has appeared in *The Dark, Cossmass Inifinities, the Young Explorer's Adventure Guide,* and elsewhere. Find her at flywithpigs.com and on twitter @akatherineblack.

HAILEY PIPER, is the 2x Bram Stoker Award-nominated author of *The Worm and His Kings, Queen of Teeth,* and other horror books. She's a member of the HWA with over seventy published short stories, including multiple appearances and one editing stint in *Planet Scumm.*

AUTHOR BIOS

HAILEY PIPER (con't): Hailing from the haunted woods of New York, she now lives with her wife in Maryland, where their paranormal research is classified. Find Hailey at www.haileypiper.com or on Twitter via @HaileyPiperSays.

PAUL C.K. SPEARS is a writer and lover of the weird and occult living in Cranston, Rhode Island. He has previously been published in *Weirdbook Magazine* ("Witches" edition, 2017) and the *Enter the Rebirth Apocalypse Anthology* (2018). He enjoys horror movies, tabletop roleplaying games, and doing Wikipedia deep-dives about UFO encounters.

ARTIST BIO

MAURA MCGONAGLE, whom goes by 'Moe', is a bedraggled illustrator. Being a true professional, they have been rejected from most reputable and disreputable societ-ies and were marooned in space for their crimes. Rescued by Scummy, they are now held captive (crossed out) a happy disciple with no other interests, no sir.

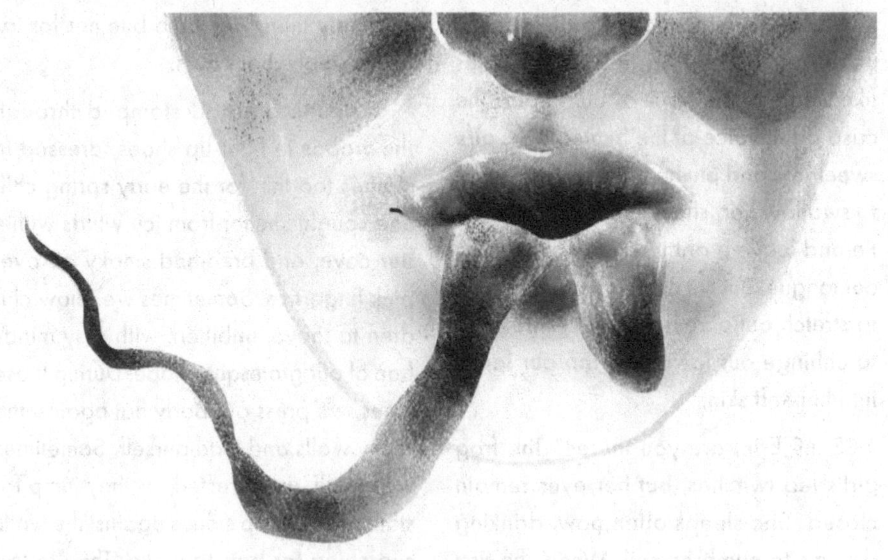

CHELSEA MUZAR

CAVE OF THE LOST FROG WOMAN

We spy the woman at the mouth of our cave. Lifted on tiptoes, with hands cupped around her eyes, she searches the darkness for the little lost frog girl. Of all the village's hunters, she is the only one close to finding the child. But she cannot enter here.

She paces, scraping fingers through snowy hair and glaring at the dripping maw of our home. We shake our body in silent laughter as the swollen cries of forest frogs saturate the air.

The frog girl shivers in the corner, where she sleeps huddled around herself, two skinny arms and legs intertwined. She whimpers as she dreams, and her dirty clothes cling to her body, sticking to knobby knees and pointed elbows.

She's been with us for three days and is beginning to fade like the others. Soon, she will be tender enough to swallow whole.

She deserves this, this cruel frog girl, with blonde hair smattered with dirt and bat droppings. She's earned this.

"Hello!"

The sound echoes, but the girl clutches to her sleep.

We slither close to the mouth of our cave, our belly dragging. A hiss rises like steam at the back of our throat. The crisp adult voice of the hunter lacks airy sweetness and plump naivety. If we were to swallow her, she'd taste like bitter nettle and leave a gritty residue of spite on our tongue. But we cannot leave our cave to stretch out across the rocky threshold, to unhinge our jaw and snap our fangs into her soft skin.

"Erin? Erin, are you there?" The frog girl's leg twitches, but her eyes remain closed. She sleeps often now, drinking dreams to numb herself. When she first entered our cave and found our scaled body, she was all shrill screams and fearful clawing hands. Now she's silent breathing and soft shuffling limbs. We like it better this way, the quiet obedience of it.

"Is anybody in there?" the hunter calls.

She will have to come inside if she wants the child; then we will sink our poisoned fangs into her neck and send her back to town, where she will die dreaming about our monstrous shape. She must know this because she hesitates at the lip of our cave.

We flick our forked tongue, smelling the worry on her breath, then slink toward the corner and the curled body sleeping there. We wrap our tail around the child's bare foot and imagine crushing it. Pain would rip the girl from her slumber. Surely then, as screams coat our cave, the white-haired hunter would rush in.

Surely then, we could bite her for trying to steal what's ours.

The little girl had stomped through the woods in light-up shoes, dressed in clothes too thin for the early spring chill. She sought shelter from icy winds within our cave, and breathed smoky air over pink fingertips. Sometimes we allow children to leave, unbitten, with rosy minds free of our grotesque shape. During those times, we press our body flat against the rocky walls and hide ourself. Sometimes we watch, uninterested, as they jump for stalactites or skip stones against the walls, searching for bats to wake. They're too afraid of the swarm descending to throw pebbles at the ceiling, but they love to feign bravery, so their rocks beat our walls, and echo like rain.

This time we were not interested in the little girl or her dancing shoes. We were tired and rested coiled around dark stalagmites. Not even her fresh skin or sweet voice aroused our hunger. If she had left our cave after warming her hands and done her cruel deed elsewhere, then she would've made it back to her warm, dry home. But she did not leave, and now she is trapped here.

"I know you're in there," the white-haired woman says. It does not matter that she knows, she must come in if she wants the frog child. We give the pale foot a little squeeze, not hard enough to wake the girl. Not yet.

"I know you're in there, Aliyah."

That name echoes off our walls and shrivels us. We crush the foot and the girl rises screaming from her sleep. She claws at our tail, mouth wrenched open and crooked teeth exposed. There's a crunch of bone, and the screaming becomes shrill. We almost don't hear the boot clicking across the entrance.

We release the sobbing child and race toward the opening of our cave, mouth already unhinged, but all we find is a discarded black boot thrown a few feet past the entrance. Our fangs retreat, and our tongue flicks out. It stinks of muddy plastic, feet and something else—the crisp smell of fresh snow. The muted scent of winter is strange, since spring has just opened her arms.

"I'm going to need that back eventually, Aliyah, but for now you may keep it."

The woman stands with her hands clasped behind her back. Her pale neck is splotched red with worry. She's smiling, but staring in a direction where we are not. It's purposeful, this fake stare, because her eyes drift toward us only to snap back into place.

How does she know that name? A name which hasn't been spoken in the forest for centuries. A name replaced with devil snake, beldame, and cursed serpent of the caves. Those who knew that name have long since perished.

We pick up the boot with the end of our tail and place it just beyond her reach, a few steps into our cave. In the thin strips of sunlight, our dark green scales are dull and several bald patches are covered in stretched skin. We'll never get rid of that skin, leeched of color from the years trapped in darkness. No matter how many times we rub ourself raw against jagged rocks, we were not born in this body, and we cannot shed our human skin completely.

"You don't need the girl, Aliyah, any more than you need that serpent inside you," the hunter says. We shudder. That name presses us flat against the damp floor. She stares at us now, at our misshapen head and stretched body. The end of our tail, flattened toes glued into a perfect point, curls close to our side.

If she is afraid of us, her face does not reveal it, though she plucks at the edge of her shirt. "Release her, Aliyah."

"Exchange." The word stumbles on our forked tongue. We say it again, afraid she cannot understand.

"Eating me won't help you." She removes her other boot and tosses it to the side. She tugs her white hair into a ponytail. The hair is like that of an old woman, but her face is round and young. She rolls up the ends of her pants and shrugs off her jacket. White tattoos coil around her arms and spiral up her shoulders. "It won't change you back, and it won't complete your transformation."

"We do not believe you." We can smell her better now that she's exposed more of her skin. She isn't fragranced like us, of dewy rock and stale shadow, but she doesn't stink like the frog girl either, of sticky chocolate, sour teeth, and creamy lotion. She smells like frozen earth. A winter woman.

"Fair point." From her pocket she withdraws a bundle of herbs, wrapped tightly with pieces of green cord. "I'm here to help you, but I need the girl first. I can't allow you to have her."

"You do not command us." Our tongue trips on the *S* and drags it into a hiss. "Human, but not human, we were a little girl once too."

We were a normal girl once, when we lived in town, a small village back then. We wore the same dress everyday, a white one our grandmother had spun. We wore it down into a dull yellow-gray, with brown stains on the hem from cave mud. We always loved exploring the caves that haunted the forest. They hummed with tranquility, echoing the pings of water droplets, and the soft rustling of bat wings. They were welcoming places, or that's what we believed. We had been innocent once.

The winter woman steps closer and we reel back, ready to strike. She raises her hand. "Don't listen to the snake anymore."

The girl, whose foot is broken, crawls on her stomach, sobbing in pain. Her belly slides across the mud as she comes closer to the mouth of our cave, drawn to the woman's voice, and the hope of being saved.

We flatten ourself against the wall and wait for the child to move closer to the threshold. We will eat her in front of this woman, then she will learn, just as we have learned, the violent truth about caves. The winter woman understands our plan and she holds up her hands. "Aliyah, don't!"

The girl, blinded by exhaustion, doesn't register the winter woman's distress.

"Mommy," she begs, her voice thin from dehydration. She is a small child, with curly hair that sits in tangled piles atop her head. When she entered our cave, her cheeks held a faint pink tint, but now they are chalky white and streaked with mud.

Our tail lashes out and snags the girl off the ground. A shrill wail spirals through the air, and we dangle her upside down, shaking her until she stops screaming. A thin line of drool falls from her mouth as her eyes roll back.

"She deserves it." We hiss and lick her sunken face with the edge of our tongue.

🗵

When the child first entered our cave, she removed a frog from her jacket pocket, and held the twitching creature in unsteady hands. She knelt on damp soil and searched our floor for smooth, flat stones. Water slipped down rock icicles and dripped into small pools, as blue and red lights flashed in the darkness.

We lifted our head and watched as a stone was dropped onto the frog. The frog

CAVE OF THE LOST FROG WOMAN

screamed, a banshee *REEEEEE!*, and the girl flinched. She shared uncertain giggles with the chittering bats and stared, mesmerized, at the screaming animal. Mocking, she screeched like a piglet. She laughed openly then.

She used another rock to crush the frog's legs; this time grinding stone against wet skin. The frog crawled, with broken legs, toward the sunlight drifting into our cave. The child stood up and stomped her shoes beside the frog's head, stirring up more screams and childish laughter. Her shoe lights strobed as we slithered out of our hiding place and raised ourself high, our long neck kissing the ceiling. Her laughter wilted when she saw the shadow of us looming above her. She screamed when we opened our wide mouth and clicked our fangs into place. She ran, but she was in our cave and we didn't let her leave.

We ate the frog, to end its suffering.

⧗

"She deserves this," we say again, and slip the unconscious child's foot into our mouth.

"Like you deserved it?"

The woman lights her herb stick and steps into our cave. Foolish woman, if she thinks a little sage can cleanse us. Others have tried and failed. We are more powerful than any village dweller. But we are not stupid, we sense her power too. A magic like ours, but faint, smaller.

We drop the child and shake our body in joyful laughter. We will eat this woman, absorb her frozen essence, and use her magic to leave our cave. Then we won't have to rely on the foolish ones who wander too close to our home. We will slither down to the village that cursed us, enter their safe, dry houses and swallow them as they sleep. Their homes will become ours, and they will finally see us. They won't be able to turn their faces away.

Smoke from the herbs rises to the ceiling and stirs the bats. Screeches echo as they beat their wings and flee our cave in a massive cloud. In their panic, they ram into our head, clawing at our face and bulbous eyes. Blinded, we hiss and slam ourselves against the jagged wall, before dropping low to the safety of the cold, damp soil.

We cannot see the woman, but we can hear her feet slapping against the ground, her labored breath beside us—to the right! We swipe our tail and graze an ankle. The sound of fluttering bats blurs the map in our mind, but it's all right.

The hunter's in our cave; we will find her before she can make it to the entrance.

We hear the herbs tossed aside, and the rough grabbing of the unconscious child. The winter woman slips and lands hard, cursing. We follow the sounds and peel our arms away from our body to grab her, but our hands are clumsy and weak from years of uselessness. Our fingers thread through brittle hair, unable to close around it and pull the woman into our mouth. We scamper after her, limping on our hands, when we touch something that burns our skin.

Smoke hits our face, and the smell of burning flesh, sage, mint and tobacco overwhelms us. Memories of the old village invade our mind. There's the dusty brown paths we used to take through the forest on our journeys to the caves and home again.

There's our grandmother, sitting in her chair, a switch resting across her lap. A smoking pipe clenched between her teeth, and her thin lips wrinkled with disgust.

Our grandmother's face turned a purplish-red when she grew cross, and she looked more beet than human. She always smelled of tobacco, sage, and mint. Even after bathing in the river, where I slapped her clothes against the rocks a hundred times to beat away the dirt. The smell worked its way into the folds of her skin and never faded.

Inside our cave, blurry images surface: puddles of muddy water, a pair of boots on the ground. We shake our head to focus, but it is no use, so we keep our eyes closed. With the bats gone, we can hear the child breathing in the bowels of this place. The winter woman has foolishly wandered into the belly of our home. We will show this stranger what happens to those who wander into *our* cave. We dip low against the floor and use our hands to propel our massive body forward.

"Aliyah, release the snake! You don't need it anymore." The winter woman's voice echoes on the walls, bouncing in all directions, but we know where she's hiding. We follow the scent of decay to where we've stored the remains of the others. In the beginning it was too difficult for us to open our mouth wide and swallow them whole. We had to peel pieces off and gum them until they were soft enough to gulp down.

The girl sleeps in a nest of dirt and rocks, ignorant of the bones that linger so close to her curved back. Bruises have settled around her eyes, and she breathes so lightly her chest barely rises at all. She's not quite ripe, but we will have her now anyway.

There's a sudden, icy chill on our back. "Aliyah!"

The winter woman stands behind us, the tattoos on her arms glowing faintly.

"What has she honestly done? She's a child—"

"She killed a frog." I wrap my tail around the girl's thin leg and drag her out of her mud bed. "She crushed its legs and laughed. She deserves this."

⧗

On the night I transformed, Grandmother threaded her gnarled hands in my hair and led me like a wild dog through the forest.

"I know what you've done," she hissed, smattering my face with droplets of tobacco stained saliva. A vein throbbed in her forehead as she spoke. "You think I don't know what you're doing out here for hours on hours, but I know what you're searching for. You won't find it in these forests. There's no magic here for you, Witch. You can't poison me."

"Please, Grandmother!" I cried, clutching my hair at the roots, trying to alleviate the pain, "I haven't done this!"

I was a child then, not old enough to bleed like a woman, and I prayed to the gods of air and earth one of the villagers would hear my cries and come to stop Grandmother. Just one, I prayed, squeezing my eyes closed when Grandmother slapped me across the face. Just one.

When we reached the cave, Grandmother beat me with her meaty fists until I couldn't stand. She cursed me for a demon and tied my hands to a rocky tower growing from the cave's floor. She

gave me a choice because I was her only granddaughter. Even though I was the wicked thing who killed my mother during childbirth, I was still her kin.

"Hands or feet," she asked me, spitting a glob of her tobacco on the ground. Panicked, I said nothing, so she slapped me and shouted, "Hands or feet!"

I chose feet. She spread my legs out as far as they would go.

"This is what your mother looked like when you split her," she said. She stunk of mint, sweat, and sour liquor. I kicked my legs and squirmed against the ropes around my wrists, but Grandmother stood tall and slammed her fat foot against my calf. She kicked me until I stopped moving, then she crushed my feet with thick stones. The pain was so great I'd believed myself already dead. She brought the stones down again and again, shattering my feet.

"Now you can't go walking," she laughed. "The devil inside you might have killed your mother, but it'll never get me." This is what always made Grandmother angry with me. If I didn't bring the water in quickly enough, or I served her a cold dinner, or I looked at her with my mother's whore face, she'd punish me. "You've got a wickedness inside you," she'd tell me, because I'd been born a murderer.

"This'll teach you, this'll teach you," Grandmother chanted as she knelt over me and pinched my nose until I opened my mouth to breathe. She dug out my tongue with her sweaty fingers, pressed it flat and used a knife to slice it in two. "You've earned this, witch. With your whoring to the devil."

My mouth filled with so much blood I felt trapped underwater, unable to breathe. I flexed my hands and yanked on the binding around my wrists, but the rope only dug in tighter.

I remember her voice, raging above my head, cursing me as my split tongue slipped between her fingers. She left me there, trapped inside the cave, while she fumbled her way back to the village and the little hut we had shared.

The winter woman is quiet as she watches my mouth unhinge and stretch wide enough to slip the demon frog girl inside. "You're right," she says, holding up her hand. "Aliyah, you're right. She shouldn't have killed the frog."

Her voice is sweet honey, like the little snake's voice who visited us in the cave where I was dying.

⧗

"I can help you, weak little frog," the snake had said as it slithered up my stomach. It paused below my cheek, lifting its small head and flicking its tongue. "What? You think you are not a frog? Then why are your feet so flat?"

It shook its head side to side, laughing, then continued to travel up my body.

I'd heard stories of shifters in the woods, demons who stalked to the village at night, preying on sheep and pigs. In the stories, they were always wolves and bears. No one said anything about a blue and red snake.

"I can make you strong," It cooed. "I can make it so no one can ever hurt you again."

Before I could protest, it wriggled into my wounded mouth, slid down my throat and rested inside my belly. It felt warm, like blue-fire flames licking my insides.

The snake transformed me into something stronger. My legs were useless, unable to hold me up, so it used my hands and

CAVE OF THE LOST FROG WOMAN

pierced my broken feet with pine needles, sewing them together into a point, and glued my thighs together with tree sap.

I learned to crawl on my belly and never relied on my hands. The snake knocked out all of my teeth and replaced them with a pair of sharp, yellow fangs. Patches of scales erupted on my thighs, back and arms. My forked tongue suited my new appearance, and I thanked Grandmother as I coiled myself at the entrance of my new home.

⧗

"How can I help you, Aliyah?" the winter woman asks. She steps closer, her fingers spread, ready to touch my scales. Her tattooed arms are supple, womanly, so different from a child's.

We toss the frog girl, then strike, sinking our fangs into the meat of the winter woman's arm. We release our poison into her body. Soon she will become soft and lifeless, and we will consume her and the weak frog girl together. Soon we will shed our human skin entirely, and become something stronger, with no memories of our mortal past, and even the scent of Grandmother will mean nothing to us anymore.

Suddenly there's a pain in our mouth. Icy pain that digs into our gums. We rear back and shake our head until the bones blur into the walls, but the pain doesn't stop. The ice spreads inside us, down our throat, into our lungs and stomach, and the sewn points of our feet. Our body slams into the rock, until finally we go numb and slip onto the floor of our cave. Writhing on the ground, we glare at the winter woman, who appears unfazed by our venomous bite.

"You can't eat me, Aliyah," she says, with the same pity of those villagers who gossiped about Grandmother and me. They knew what Grandmother was doing, but we were as good as strangers to them, cloistered at the edge of the wood.

"Why?" The winter woman isn't poisoned. She smells so much colder now, stronger.

"We're peas, you and me," she says, tracing her tattoos with her fingertips. "This wasn't a gift either."

She's the same as us. So she knows the child deserves to be eaten. Why is she standing in our way? Our head is fogged with frost and every time we breathe the icicles inside our lungs shake.

"She killed the frog."

"She's only a child," the winter woman says, taking a step toward the girl, "just as you were a child."

"Children are capable of terrible things. She crushed its feet, and that creature had done nothing to deserve such violence. It was innocent and she tortured it." Something slithers inside our stomach. We press our head against the wall of the cave and rock back and forth, scraping our scalp with ridged stones. "She tortured it, for hours. She made sure no one would ever want to touch it again, so it couldn't become a little whore like its mother."

Rocks tremble as we smash our head against the walls to skewer the memories and drag them from our mind. "I was a harmless frog and she murdered me."

A stalactite dances above the child's legs. Her blonde hair is completely brown now, coated with dust, and her eyes are open, glossy and unfocused. She breathes slowly, through cracked lips, and scratches at the floor with broken fingernails. She's not yet a woman, with a flat frame and round face.

She's fragile, like Grandmother's beautiful clay tobacco pipe, the one with the red poppies painted along the side. The one I accidentally knocked off the table and shattered into a dozen jagged pieces on the day she took me to the cave. The child's hands are small and gray. Her broken foot twists in the wrong direction.

"Mommy…" she whispers, her voice barely a scratch in her throat. Then she closes her eyes so tight, as if she's wishing for someone, anyone to come save her.

"She's only a child," we say, and the thing writhing in our stomach shoots up our throat.

"You were only a child," the winter woman says.

We buckle forward and retch, and the blue and red snake, once the size of a strip of ribbon, now the length of a man, tears from my mouth and thrashes on the ground. It opens its mouth wide, revealing two sharp fangs, ready to strike, but the winter woman is faster. She grabs it by the back of its head and squeezes. The snake, which has lived inside me for centuries, crumbles into tobacco ash.

The winter woman wipes the dust on her pants, then squats beside Erin. She strokes the child's head and offers her a drink from the slender mouth of a bottle.

"It's all right," she says, "you'll be home soon. Rest, rest."

My body quivers. Without the snake, I am nothing but a hastily sewn patchwork of scales and skin. I curl myself around a broken stalagmite as the trembling worsens. There's a shadow above me, and fear seizes me when I see Grandmother, with her beet face and her switch. But it's the winter woman who touches me; her icy skin soothes the ache in my misshapen skull.

"It's done now," she says, tracing my scales with the gentle tips of her fingers, "it's over."

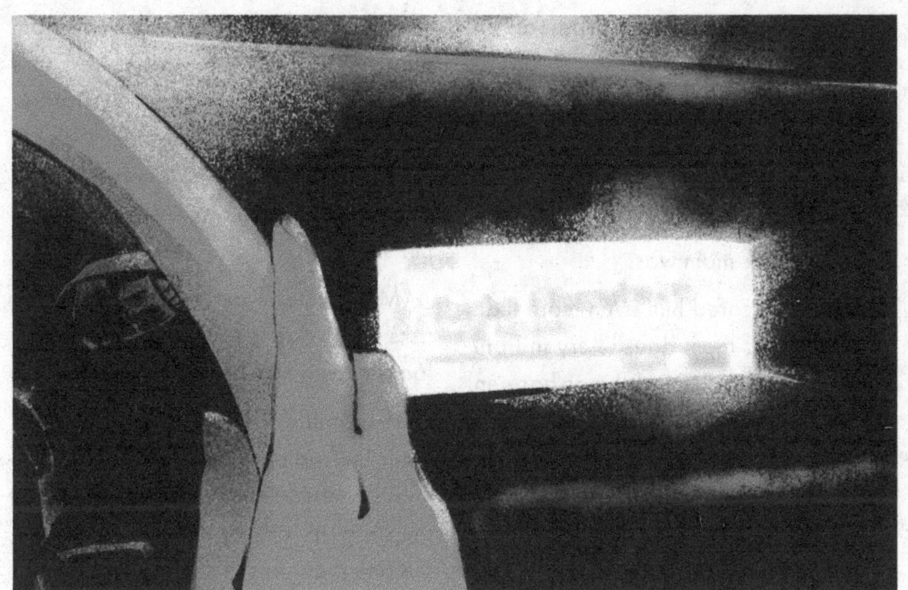

LINDSAY KING-MILLER

RADIO ELSEWHERE

Aiden wakes up in the back seat of the car. It's really dark outside. He feels like they're going fast, but it's hard to tell when he can't see their surroundings. They must be driving through the mountains, far from the city lights. It takes an hour to get to the mountains from Aiden's house. He slept for a long time.

There's a feeling in Aiden's chest, a bad, scared, *wrong* feeling. He thinks it's been there since Mom first came and got him from his bed, however many hours ago that was. It hurts, makes it hard to breathe.

When Mom shook him awake, there was something wrong with her face. It was dark except for his Mike Wazowski nightlight, so he couldn't figure out why she looked weird at first. Then he realized her nose was messed up, squashed across her face like a lump of Play-Doh. A moment later he saw the blood.

Aiden has always known about Mom and Luke. He knows not to trust Luke even when Luke pretends to be nice. He's seen bruises and band-aids on his mom lots of times. But she's never come into his room with blood on her face before. Must've been really bad if she didn't have time to wash her face.

Mom scooped him up and carried him like a little kid, still in his pajamas, his legs around her waist and head on her shoulder.

"I've got you," she whispered into his hair as she carried him down the stairs. "Shh, baby, I've got you," as if he was having a tantrum. Except Aiden wasn't crying, and his mom was.

The tears scared him even more than the blood. His mom doesn't cry in front of him. When really sad things happen, she laughs this not-funny laugh, shakes her head, and stares off into the distance.

"That's hard," she says, and sometimes she adds "Like something out of an Angie McLeod song."

Angie McLeod used to be his mom's name. Her old name, before Luke came along and gave her his name and then gave her Aiden and then she was stuck with both of them.

She's never said it like that, but Aiden understands. If it weren't for him, she would have shaken Luke off like the dirt from her work boots in that song she used to sing. The purple circles under her eyes, the fingernail marks on her arms, her one tooth that used to be pointy but now is broken off flat: all those things happened because Aiden was born.

There's an album cover in a picture frame, like it used to hang on a wall somewhere, but now it's on the floor in the closet, behind a shoe rack. In the picture, Aiden's mom is in the front seat of a pickup truck, sticking her feet out the window. She's wearing the dirty work boots from the song. The boots are in focus; his mom's face—Angie McLeod's face—is farther from the camera and blurry. It's the only picture Aiden knows of where Angie is smiling, and you can't even really see her smile.

"Mom, where are we going?" Aiden asks. It's so dark outside the car. Nothing looks even a little familiar.

His mom doesn't answer for a long time. The radio is playing, low and staticky, but after a minute Aiden recognizes the song. It's one of his mom's favorites, the one that goes "I shot a man in Reno just to watch him die." The singer's voice sounds like a car going over railroad tracks. Sometimes Aiden says this out loud and his mom laughs, but right now he keeps the thought inside his head.

"I'm sorry, baby," she says, after so long that Aiden's mostly forgotten he asked a question. Her voice is so quiet and so sad. "I couldn't leave you there with him."

⬚

Aiden remembers hearing Mom and Luke after he went to bed—last night, or maybe the night before.

"You won't," Luke said, and "I will," said Angie, and then Luke said "Try if you want, but no judge is going to give you custody of my son."

Angie tried to say something else, but Luke cut her off. "How long's it been since you held down a job? You're going to support that boy on the residuals from one shitty yeehaw album?"

Whatever Angie said after that was too quiet for Aiden to hear, but Luke's response was perfectly audible. "I don't give a shit what you do," he said, "but if you take him, I'll come after you."

Aiden didn't sleep well after he heard that. Mom going away and leaving him with Luke would be the worst thing. He tries not to be alone in the house with Luke if he can help it, and Angie notices, sets up playdates for him at his friends' houses when she needs to go somewhere by herself. Luke doesn't act the same way with him as he does with Angie; he's never hit Aiden, never thrown anything more at him than a sharp look, but Aiden is terrified of him all the same.

The Reno song is over and a new one comes on, something Aiden doesn't recognize. He doesn't like it as much, either. This singer has a higher, angrier voice. It's like they're yelling, trying to get someone to listen to them.

Aiden doesn't like yelling. "Mom, can we change the radio?" he asks.

She glances back at him in the rearview mirror. All he can see are her eyes. "This is the only station that will come in," she tells him.

"Can we put on a CD? Or that podcast where they talk about science?"

"No, baby," she says. "We don't have any of that stuff with us."

"Not even your phone?"

"Not even my phone."

She sounds really sad, so Aiden doesn't throw a fit, even though he wishes she had stopped to grab a few things. Some of his books, his movies. Feeling around him in the backseat, he realizes he doesn't even have his stuffed kangaroo, which he was definitely holding when Mom got him out of bed. He dropped it on the stairs, maybe. He doesn't remember.

There was too much going on when they left the house. Angie's nose bleeding, crying in his hair, and Luke on the stairs behind them, his face huge and white. He wasn't yelling, but he was still scary. He looked at Angie and Aiden and he said, "You don't have anywhere to go."

"Fuck you," Angie said over Aiden's head.

"You'll be back," Luke told her. "And if you're not, I'll find you."

"Fuck you," Angie said again, still crying, which was something else she didn't do usually—cuss in front of Aiden. He'd heard her say that to Luke before, but only through walls, never when Aiden was right in the room.

⌧

"Who's this singing?" he asks now.

Maybe the screaming person—the voice is in a weird range where it could be a man or a woman—is someone who would understand Aiden, who'd know how freaked out and confused he is right now. Aiden feels a little like screaming, too.

"It's Kurt Cobain," his mother says. "He was really young."

That's a weird thing to say, Aiden thinks. Everyone was really young one time, until they weren't anymore.

Aiden tries again to look out the window. Part of the problem is his head won't turn all the way. His neck hurts, probably from sleeping in the car. All he can see

in the glass is his own reflection, and not even the whole reflection of his face, just his eyes. They look big and heavy, which is also how they feel, too big for his face and too tired to stay open. But he doesn't want to go back to sleep. He wants to see where they're going.

Finally Aiden realizes why it's so dark. "Mom, you don't have your headlights on."

The road in front of them is pitch black. It's incredible that they've made it this far without hitting something—or have they? Aiden has a dim half-memory of some kind of thud, an impact in his bones, before he woke up. Maybe his mom ran over a raccoon or something while he was sleeping.

His stomach twists. Maybe it wasn't a raccoon. He thinks of his friend Jersey's dog, who dug under the fence and got hit by a car in the street right in front of their house. He hopes if they hit anything, it was a raccoon. He doesn't want to imagine a kid like Jersey walking outside in the morning to find their dog all squashed in a puddle of dry blood.

"Mom, your headlights," Aiden says again.

"They won't turn on," Angie tells him.

"How can you see where you're going?"

"I know where I'm going," she says heavily. Kurt Cobain stops singing, which is both a relief and maybe kind of a disappointment, because Aiden was starting to get used to him, to get a feel for him.

Another song comes on, this one old-sounding, a crackly recording of a woman with a crackly voice, singing something sad with a piano backing her up. The sound of her crooning for her baby to come back is somehow more unsettling than Kurt Cobain's ragged screams. Then his mom starts singing along, and that's worse. It's way worse, because Angie sounds so sad, and Aiden's really scared she's going to start crying again.

He tries to find her eyes again in the rear-view, to see if they have tears in them. Angie won't look back at him. She keeps her gaze fixed on the blackness beyond the car, and she sings, and Aiden can't see her face at all.

He wants to know where they're going. Didn't he already ask? But she didn't answer him—or maybe she did and he forgot about it already. The feeling that he missed something important is growing steadily worse. It's like the time he fell asleep in the movie theater, and when he woke up everyone was shooting at each other and he didn't know which ones were the bad guys. That's how it feels now, like everything is loud and angry and violent and he doesn't know who wants to hurt him and who wants to protect him.

Except everything is quiet and sad, and there's no one in the car except him and his mom, who would do anything in the world to keep him safe. So how is it the same?

Aiden tries to close his eyes. Maybe he can fall back asleep, and when he wakes up again they'll be at a hotel or a friend's house or a campsite or wherever his mom has in mind. He thinks about that, imagines waking up in a soft bed, or on a couch covered with pillows.

His head lolls back against the headrest and his mind starts to drift. Maybe he'll wake up with a blanket over him, soft and warm, threadbare from long use. He can almost feel it tucked up to his chin, protecting him, but then he turns his head and the blanket is covering his face, and it's dark and he can't breathe and he jerks upright again.

"Mom," he half-shouts. "Mom."

Angie doesn't answer him for a moment. Then, like before, she says "I'm sorry, baby."

"Is he following us?"

His mom does her not-funny laugh. "He's not following us anywhere," she says. "Not anymore."

The scary feeling in Aiden's chest is getting worse and worse. Something bad happened before he woke up in the backseat. Somewhere between the bottom of the stairs and out here in the dark, something happened that he missed, that he's forgetting. Something really important,

something that explains why they're still driving, why they can't stop for the night. Why they can't stop. *Will they ever stop?*

"Where are we, Mom?"

She says nothing.

"I want to go home," he says. "Mom, we shouldn't have to leave. We can throw him out. It's *our* house. I want to go home, I want—I want— "

It's hard to breathe, his throat tight around the thought of *everything*, all his books and toys and the stuffed kangaroo, probably still on the stairs where he dropped it. He can't stand to think of it just lying there all by itself, but the thought of Luke picking it up is even worse.

"There's nowhere to turn around out here," she says. "This road only goes one way."

⌛

Aiden remembers Luke saying, "If you leave, he'll never forgive you. Boy grows up without a mother, that's a wound that never heals."

What his mom is saying now sounds like sort of the same thing: something that can't be taken back, a door that once closed will never open again. He remembers Luke's hand on his arm, trying to pull him out of his mother's grasp. Aiden screamed then, wailing like a little baby and not even caring, wrapping Angie tight in his legs and arms so they couldn't be separated.

"No!" he'd yelled. "No no no!"

Angie had screamed too. And she'd pushed, hadn't she?

Aiden remembers now. He didn't see anything, his eyes were squeezed so tight, his face buried in Angie's shoulder, but he heard her grunt, the sharp exhale that stirred the tiny hairs on his cheek. There was a flat, heavy sound. It reminded Aiden of when Jersey ran in front of him while he was swinging, and their bodies collided with a thud that knocked the air out of him. When Angie pushed Luke, that sound was followed by a sharper *whack*, some hard part of a human body hitting something much harder.

"Bitch," he remembers Luke saying, shock and rage and pain all twisted together in his voice. Aiden might not have recognized it if he didn't already know it was Luke talking. "You fucking *bitch*. I'm gonna—"

"Don't come near me," Angie said, and it was like she was trying to sound scary, like when she told Aiden to do his homework *right now young man*, except her voice was too small.

"It doesn't matter," Luke said. "I'm calling the cops. I'll tell them you attacked me and stole my car. How far do you think you'll get before they find you?"

"Shut up," Angie said.

"They're gonna take him away from you," Luke said, and Aiden screamed *no no no* again, but this time only in his head.

He's screaming *no no no* in his head now, too.

⬙

"Mom, what happened?" he asks. "Why can't we go back?"

He wants to see her face, to watch her eyes and the corners of her mouth so he knows she's telling the truth. He searches for her in the rearview mirror, but it's so dark and she's just a blur. Aiden's chest hurts so bad. So, so bad.

He doesn't see her reach for the dial, but the song on the radio gets louder. This one he definitely recognizes. His mom listened to it all the time a couple years ago, when the singer's face was all over the news because she hanged herself in a hotel room. It's a pretty song, but Aiden doesn't like it. The dead girl's pretty voice makes him feel worse.

"These songs don't go together," he says. "What station are we even listening to?"

"After a certain time of night," Angie tells him, "the radio only plays songs by people who have died."

"Turn it off," Aiden says. "I don't like it."

"You'll get used to it," Angie says.

He wonders when she turned the radio on, because there was no music playing when they pulled out of the driveway, Aiden knows that for sure. All he could hear then was Angie crying and swearing, tires squealing as she hit the gas too hard.

⬙

"Fuck him, fuck him, fuck him," she'd chanted, and when he looked in the rearview he saw her nose smashed and bleeding, her eyes full of tears.

"Mom, your headlights," he'd said then, just like he said it a minute ago, but Angie didn't seem to hear him.

She looked back at him in the mirror for a long time. Too long to have her eyes off the road.

"Mom?" Aiden said.

"I'm sorry, baby," said Angie. "I love you." And after that, Aiden woke up in the backseat.

⌛

The radio plays a twangy guitar riff. Aiden recognizes it. Usually it makes him feel happy, free, like riding his bike down a big hill, but now it makes his chest hurt more, right in the place where his voice would come from if he started singing along. It's that Angie McLeod song, the one about the dirty boots.

I'll scrape you off and send you home, but I'll be rolling on, his mother croons.

Maybe his eyes are adjusting to the darkness, or maybe the sun is coming up, but for the first time, Aiden realizes he can see other cars on the road with them. One is close enough that Aiden could make eye contact with the driver, if they turned their head, but Aiden doesn't think they will. He can't imagine there's enough muscle left to turn. Aiden knows why his chest hurts now, but he doesn't look down at himself to confirm it.

He knows what he would see.

Instead, he looks for Angie in the rearview mirror one more time. Now that there's light to see by, he realizes that her face doesn't look very much like her face. Her eyes are the same, but everything else is red and smashed up, sparkling with little pieces of broken glass and bone.

One more time, she says, "I'm sorry."

Aiden doesn't say *it's okay*. He leans his head against the window and listens to the dead woman singing on the radio.

ELI WILKINSON

FERTILIZER

The contents of this document are intended for investigators and superiors with DIRECT involvement in the Dean Soper investigation. Authorization from Deputy Chief Constable Allison Miller is required to read further.

The following has been transcribed from a notebook recovered from the Marble Arch Hotel, referred to hereafter as the Marble Arch Hotel Notebook (MAHN). Accounts, claims, corrections, and references have been annotated as footnotes for clarity. Grammar and hand-made corrections have been edited for clarity. Syntax and underlines have been maintained and indicate the author's emphasis.

PLEASE BE ADVISED: Document's original author is wanted for questioning in the Dean Soper investigation[1].

🕳

MAY 24TH

I am sure I have found it.

The specimen is in a sidewalk plot just off Carall Street, down west Pender, situated

---

1   Name on the inside cover is *Iustus Vultus*. Investigators could not verify the name with hotel staff or witnesses. Address and apartment number are to the Marble Arch Hotel. Given later references to "Vic" or "Dr. Vic," it is assumed this name is another of the suspect's aliases.

directly in front of a new condominium complex—part of widespread redevelopment in the area.

While the west end of Pender Street is now characterized by cookie-cutter urban architecture—glass and steel condominiums squatting upon boutique shops—east and north of the street are still rightly considered rough parts of town. From a predatory perspective the neighbourhood is perfect, a Darwinian crucible for all manner of hunting and parasitic lifeforms.

The street is home to many affluent young professionals. I have interviewed a number of them, and they seem more concerned with their "sketchy" and "ghetto" neighbours than they are with the high number of deaths and disappearances in the area. Looking at census data I estimate the number of people living in this renewed two-to-three block radius to be somewhere around 700 or so. Conversely, a few blocks north, there are no official figures on the number of permanent residents—estimates put it at around 6,000 and, based on my own observations, this seems correct. There appears to be a higher percentage of males and seniors, all mostly confined to the SRO hotels common to the area.

Though I have found conflicting reports on the subject, it seems safe to say most of the residents have some kind of mental illness. Drug use is common and open. Despite these issues, the community has a remarkable degree of solidarity. Residents have formed a number of organizations, even a podcast, to resist renewal efforts and organize against intrusions into their space. Is this why the specimen is located in a more secure neighbourhood?

While mutual aid is a strong adaptive feature, sickliness in the wild is an irresistible dinner bell, and as I argued in my dissertation, it is wishful thinking to believe the wilds and the city are somehow separate.

It is the specimen's flowers that make it a mark of interest. Each one possesses five to eight petals that are a vibrant pink, which turn a darker red nearer the fuzzy yellow carpel. These emerge from round, glaucous green bulbs nearly identical to those of *Papaver somniferum*[2] save for the length of the stalk. The rest of the specimen could easily be mistaken for a conventional *Buxus sempervirens*.[3] Unlike either species, the leaves, as I discovered the hard way, are covered in thin stinging hairs that've reddened the skin on my right hand. I hope this doesn't cause a rash[4].

Beneath the leaves, however, lies the real treasure. There are possibly thousands

---

2   *An opium plant.*

3   *Common boxwood tree.*

4   *Multiple witness reports from Marble Arch residents and the concierge recall the suspect's rash, describing it as eczema.*

of thin green vines that look something akin to Twizzler liquorice hanging from the trunk and branches of the bush. Took several photos for later study[5].

Worth noting. I am in an exceptionally good mood, a euphoria I believe might be the result of prolonged closeness to the specimen's flowers. The residents in and around the specimen seem to be in similarly good spirits.

<u>Do the flowers lure in victims? If so, how does feeding occur?</u>

Few overdoses reported on this street lead me to suspect this is not the case, however floral baiting would be consistent with descriptions in Wollheim, Buel, or Stead[6,7]. However, these cases were all documented in remote areas. I strongly doubt the specimen is a native species.

<u>How did it get here? Is its arrival a direct result of overdose spikes over the decades?</u>

These may not be answerable.

For now I plan to imbed in the community and begin preliminary interviews of what I suspect are the specimen's preferred prey.

I'm also going to try and clean this room a little—how do people live like this?

MAY 27TH

I will have to change my approach to data collection.

Doctors, even the academic kind, are apparently extremely unwelcome. I have been chased out of my first residence at the Maple and have been forced to set up at the Marble Arch under an assumed name[8]. The consensus seems, especially among the non-white residents of the neighbourhood, that all doctors are essentially an arm of the government. Given the string of overdoses and police rough housing, all outsiders—especially "bougie-ass white people"—are viewed with extreme suspicion.

Absurd. Though I can hardly blame them for that suspicion. Going to spend the next few days as the chameleon adapting to my new colours. As a young-ish woman with what I'm told aren't bad looks, I expect I will be able to slip into the population once I look the part.

JUN 1ST

Things have moved faster than I'd hoped!

---

5   *Presumably on a cellphone. No photographs recovered from suspect's room.*

6   *19th century fringe botanists who wrote accounts of human-eating plants.*

7   *Items #002-14. Investigators recovered several printed monographs with no publishing or source information indicated from the suspect's room at the Marble Arch. Subjects are cryptozoology, hypothesizing the existence of large predatory plants, including people eating vines and trees. Style mimics scientific journals. Possibly composed by the suspect.*

8   *Interviews with residents and concierge at the Maple Hotel have confirmed a "Dr. Vic" checked in and was subsequently chased out of the hotel in late May 2020. Suspect paid in cash. and gave no other names. See reports Four Horns WR - 001, Sava WR - 002, Smith WR - 003, Roberts WR - 004.*

Today I made the acquaintance of "Dirty Mike"[9]. He is a large, muscular, jovial man, with a taste for toilet humour. When I asked him how he got the name Dirty Mike, he smiled at me with the half of his teeth he has remaining, "Because I fuck a lot of bitches without condoms and shit my pants from time to time."

An appropriate sobriquet, it would seem.

Though he would present to many of the upperworld as considerably intimidating given his size, physique, and apparent uncleanliness, I could not have asked for a better Virgil to this strange and sometimes infernal ecology of poverty and psychosis. There are few people in the community he is not on a first name basis with, and he is generally liked. He was very candid with me about the abuse he suffered in childhood, and his problems with _crank_ (which I assume means some kind of amphetamine).

Aside from compulsively bathing while using (he does not wash his clothes though), he is quite diligent and watchful over the community that has become his home. He has made it clear he wishes to have sex with me.

I have of course declined, but must admit candour of this kind is very refreshing after ten years in academia. But there is also a paternal affection there.

Not wanting to be recognized after the Maple Hotel fiasco, I have adopted the persona of an extreme hypochondriac. My ruse has the added benefit of allowing me to wear a face mask even outdoors, which will hopefully prevent my being recognized,[10,11] *. Our "shared" fear of the unclean has proven a strong bonding narrative, and I am now very much under the wing of this gentle man.

His guardianship is much appreciated, as I have caught snippets of conversation about a doctor in the area asking for information regarding the specimen. Many seem to think I am somehow connected to it, though most believe there is no organism, and I am some kind of health worker trying to root out COVID-19, or else track down those who've stopped taking their medication for various mental illnesses—some kind of undercover police officer, or just a deranged freak.

Regardless of narrative, there is a running theme in wanting to stab me. I will not be seen in public without a mask

---

9   Michael Lee Four Horns.

10 Multiple descriptions of the suspect corroborate her wearing a 3-ply mask in public. Mr. Four Horns' reports he also witnessed the suspect on a few occasions without it. These interviews are the basis for the sketch of the suspect in this dossier, document 1b.

11 * Please note: Mr. Four Horns is a known user of methamphetamine and diagnosed schizophrenic. Descriptions of the suspect are inconsistent (see WR - 001). Coupled with his insistence that there is a monster living in front of the Vivian Condominiums on Pender Street, investigators doubt the validity of Mr. Four Horns description.

again, and ideally not without Mike at my side.

JUN 4TH

The city is almost completely back to normal now. Restaurants are open, people are walking about. I have to say I'm very pleased with my disguise. Dirty and loose-fitting clothes coupled with the mask make it that any person of the "upperworld" gives me a wide berth as I come down the sidewalk. I have been experimenting with odd walking styles to additional effect. Best of all, if I search an alleyway or some dark corner no one seems to care what I'm doing. I am become the perfect field researcher, completely unseen[12]. Plan on finding Mike this morning to further explore.

⧗

Could not find Mike. Returned to the room around 2:15PM, will rest and go looking for him again around 6 or 7.

JUN 5TH

Reconnected with Mike the previous evening. He apparently spent the day in an amphetamine-induced haze. He was still fairly agitated when he found me, so I tagged along mostly silently as he tried to scrounge up enough money for alcohol. By 9:30 we had hustled up enough for two tallboys. I sipped mine slowly, deliberately and discretely spilling most of it on myself to add to my disguise.

When we were done, he suggested, with no subtlety might I add, going back to my room to "sleep."

No chance—my room, my space.

He understood and did not push the topic further. Mike then suggested we seek out a friend of his who'd staked a claim to a good and dry spot for sleeping, and with no reason to decline I agreed.

Our journey took us past Pigeon Park.

It is a hub of activity in the neighbourhood. An open air market is usually open for business almost as soon as the sun is up. All manner of drugs, clothing, and assorted knick knacks are available. Central to the park's popularity as a community node is the public toilet, a stainless steel tube like something out of "Star Trek" left behind to a "Mad Max" future. I noticed no one was sleeping there, and suggested to Mike that we sleep close to the bathroom.

"You don't sleep in the park," Mike told me. *How come?*

He told me there is a "weird guy" that comes around the neighbourhood. If this person catches someone asleep or passed out on their own, those people, to use Mike's colourful phrase, "turn purple." But it is the method of the killing Mike described that I find so compelling.

To hear him tell it, this urban boogeyman injects his victims with a lethal dose

---

12 *A woman matching the suspect's description here was observed many times by Marble Arch Hotel staff, and staff of several businesses in the area rummaging through garbage.*

of heroin or other opiates, thus deflecting attention from the police. Like Wallace fever-dreaming evolution in the Malay jungle, Mike's insight into the thing is almost mystical, and like Darwin I am both alarmed and jealous that he saw it and I didn't.

Hypothesis: Can predatory mimicry become so completely adapted to an environment that prey is unaware it is being hunted?

Mike took me a few blocks east of the park to a boarded up shop with an outcropping that keeps a good portion of the sidewalk dry even in heavy rain. A man was lying in a sleeping bag in the doorway and he had a big brown dog with him that seemed friendly enough. This dog, Rusty, was sadly proof that pets do not always reflect the temperaments of their owners.

Mike carefully woke the man, who proceeded to scream and curse at him very loudly. I was very sure he would physically assault us both despite being half Mike's weight. Once calmed, at least comparatively, Mike introduced him as Angry Dean[13].

Where Mike is friendly and generally upbeat, Dean is erratic, suspicious, and—in keeping with the street's aptitude for precise nicknames—quick to anger.

Dean was adamant that he did not tolerate sluts in his presence. Sex upsets Rusty, evidently. Dean was very reluctant to give details of his life, save to say that everyone he'd ever known and loved, except faithful Rusty, had fucked him over, and that you musn't trust anyone. Despite obvious mental illness, Dean is perhaps the most legitimately ferocious person I've encountered here. Thin, but wiry, very obviously strong. His muscles are always tense, track marks on his arms and chest conjure to me images of a leopard.

It took some effort on Mike's part, but eventually he convinced Dean to share the doorway. Dean remained very reluctant, until Mike informed him that I intended to sleep in Pigeon Park near the bathroom if we were not allowed in his alcove. This more than anything changed his mind.

"Don't sleep in the park unless you have a serious death wish."

My first night of rough sleeping has left me stiff and sore. I am going to try and get some sleep before venturing back out.

JUN 8TH

Four overdoses in the last few days[14]. Two were in broad daylight. A third happened in a large group in a McDonald's bathroom. The other in a supervised injection site. I'm sure something is not right here.

Consensus among Mike, Dean, and other locals is that the resident boogeyman

---

13 AKA Decker Dean, legal name: Dean Soper. File #400634.
14 Records show only two in this time period.

is due for a visit. Everyone is extremely on edge.

On the 6th or 7th I spent most of my day observing the organism, testing my hypothesis that its flowers are a lure, hoping to perhaps identify the means and reason for its simulated overdose deaths.

I am growing confident the lure hypothesis is bust, and not just because its wonderful flowers appear to be withering up. No one from the neighbourhood came near it during my observation. Certainly not anyone likely to overdose. It is looking more and more necessary that I'll need to observe someone sleeping or unconscious on their own at night to figure out just what the hell is going on here.

I would be questioning my whole research project at this point, worrying perhaps that I am the psycho bitch my doctoral supervisor said I was. But I am sure now more than ever that the shrub in front of the Vivian Condominiums on Pender is connected to all of this. Sure because of an incident that occurred just over an hour ago.

Worried that I was in fact a loony bitch, I decided it might be prudent to do a chemical swab of the organism's flowers for later analysis. Imagine my surprise when, mid swab, I was violently pushed to the ground and screamed at by some man.

He was wearing a PPE mask, and dressed business casual. He screamed at me to leave, claimed I was ruining the neighbourhood, and said to leave the plant alone.

I have little doubt that had I not run off there would have been violence. At the end of the street I turned back to see if this man was chasing me, and observed very interesting behaviour.

He was smelling the flowers of the shrub. Practically burying his face in it. It was clear even from that distance that this relaxed him considerably. Just what this means, or where I go from here, I am not entirely sure.

JUN 12TH

Approx time 2:30. Alley between Hast + Cordov Streets, it's _wearing a disguise!_ Big dirty coat + hood, _rain poncho?_ Crusted old jeans, dirty sneakers. Motion spastic, uneven. Legs move too slow. Balances on tiptoes. Body sways at the waist, all directions. In low light easily mistaken for intoxicated or mentally ill.

Further mimicry to avoid detection?

Dog barking. Rusty may deter organism. _Did not._

2:35: Specimen has choked Rusty to death. Nauseous. Approaching Dean[15]. Has circled twice. Unlikely to wake.

Checking for observers?

15　EMS report Soper DOA Jun. 13th 2020, 9:45AM. Cause of death opioid related overdose. Investigators believe Soper strangled own dog in narcotic induced anger. Det. Lee and Lynn believe author of MAHN at minimum witnessed Soper's death and did not seek help or intervene.

Going to one knee. Hands are grey-ish green, look like loose collection of worms/palps. Hands coming apart. Thin, stringy stems. Twizzlers licorice.

Twizzler appendages entering subject through nostrils, ears, mouth.

2:40: Dean twitching but not awake.

<u>Dean gone still (2 or 3 mins later at most.)</u>

Motion under hood of poncho. (5 mins after contact approx). Hood has been pushed back. Specimen's "head" is composed of red/pink flowers.

They are so very beautiful.

FERTILIZER

Organism is pulling its hood back up and stumble/silly walking away from scene. Remarkable. Retrieved several petals for analysis[16].

JUN 13TH

Woke up late having barely slept the night before. I feel like yesterday's observations were a fever dream.

It walks. And not just that, it assumes a rough hominid shape and even wears clothing to disguise itself! There is so much here I can't even organize my thoughts, the amount of locomotion in flora, the disguise—just one of these on their own—

Hypothesis: Like other carnivorous plants, the organism supplements minerals absent from its soil through predation.

I am convinced my earlier speculation of hyperevolved mimicry is correct. The induced overdose doubles not just as a means of pacifying prey, but also obfuscates suspicion of a wolf in the sheeps' midst.

Going to leave for Pender Street in a few minutes and make further observations.

Why did it ignore me?

The specimen has returned to its plot in front of the Vivian Condominiums. Its flowers, just a day ago withered and near death, are large and bright again.

The pinks and reds of its petals are some of the most vibrant I've ever seen. The rest of the foliage is also a considerably healthier shade of green. Took several photos for later study[17].

Interestingly there is increased foot traffic in the area, and I think the specimen is responsible. During previous observations the street was relatively quiet compared to others nearby, but today the shops were busier. The cafe beside the Vivian was full (previously I have never seen more than two or three customers there at a time). The flowers could be smelt from up to about seven meters away, and everyone seemed drawn to the organism. Many couples and young women posed for pictures with it. I am still experiencing considerable euphoria that began almost as soon as I could smell its flowers.

Hypothesis: the organism's flowers may be a form of parasitism. Using upscale residents of the new condominiums to protect itself in dormancy?

It is concerning that this euphoria is still with me in spite of what happened. As I was leaving I was confronted by Mike, who was watching me from a nearby alley, and no doubt saw me taking pictures and conducting my observation.

"You didn't help him," he said, or something to that effect. I was so startled and, frankly, intoxicated, I didn't think clearly before responding.

---

16 *No flower petals recovered from the suspect's room.*

17 *Presumably on a cellphone. No photographs recovered from suspect's room.*

I said something along the lines of neither did he. Just where he was last night I have no idea.

I looked all over for him and only stopped when I came across Dean and decided to camp there and wait for him. When the organism was approaching I retreated behind a nearby recycling dumpster to conduct my observation. Mike evidently witnessed this.

(_Always, always, always check the surroundings Vic!_).

He accused me of being a government agent of some kind because he saw me writing in this book. Tried as I might he would not listen to me. Honestly, why should he have?

He was extremely agitated, and quickly became convinced the organism (which he called a monster— so crude!) must be, quote, "lit up," an expression I've never heard before. His accompanying miming made it clear he intended to set it on fire. Did my best to explain to him that arson in broad daylight on a busy street would likely end in jail time, but he had become so erratic and loud he seemed to barely process anything.

"Better to rot in fucking jail than let Audrey get my people!" is how he put it.

Who is Audrey?[18]

I did not, and still do not, wish any harm to Mike, or any other residents of this area.

They, we, are all part of a uniquely liminal ecosystem. Our world, full of artificial light and eyes, altering temperatures, and nearly incalculable pollutants is proving to be rich fertilizer for emergent properties and selections previously unseen—or perhaps species like my bouquet have always existed and are only now come to adaptive advantage. Either way, it is not in anyone's purview, certainly not anyone named Dirty Mike, to decide that this creature is to join so many others in extinction simply for inconveniencing us.

I did what I could in the moment. I scratched at his eyes and screamed rape.

Then came the whirlwind.

I know for certain we fought. I am not injured save for a few bruises and scrapes— in spite of everything I believe it was not Mike's intention to hurt me, only to get me out of the way so he could do what he had to. The only silver lining in all this is his Tennyson charge at the specimen may actually have confirmed my hypothesis of the organism using upscale residents as additional protection. No one came to my aid when Mike was on top of me, but after a few moments he tossed me aside and ran for my bouquet probably intending to stomp it or rip it up with his bare hands! Immediately, three men tackled Mike and wrestled him to the ground.

This observation could not be construed as scientific, but in my opinion they seemed possessed, almost compelled to

---

18   Det. Lee has confirmed with Mr. Four Horns that this was a reference to 'Little Shop of Horrors.'

   FERTILIZER

save the specimen. Unfortunately, given the scene I'd caused I felt discretion would be in my interest, and made my getaway just as the police were arriving.

It is clear to me now that my immersive study of the organism and its unique ecology is at an end. Today's incident was much too close a call. I have gathered all my data in my bag and I'm ready to leave as soon as I've taken swabs of the carpels of the flowers. Tonight I'll revisit the Vivian. I believe the organism will remain dormant until it needs to feed again, and a late night visit should also minimize the possibility of one the locals becoming agitated.

—TRANSCRIPTION END—

⧗

Three east side residents; Pamela Sava, of the Maple Hotel; Annie Johnston; and Anthony Paull, were arrested for breaking into room 505 of the Marble Arch Hotel.

In her statement, Sava testified her belief that the suspect was conducting experiments on vulnerable east side residents[19]. The suspect was not present, and Sava, Johnston, and Paull's break-in precipitated the 911 call from the hotel's concierge.

Responding officers McRae and Swartz discovered the MAHN and contacted Homicide. Suspect last seen on foot, heading west down Hastings Street towards downtown core.

A complete inventory of evidence recovered from the Marble Arch Hotel room 505 is attached to this file. This transcript is to be kept with the arrest report of Mr. Four Horns.

Charges against Mr. Four Horns are pending as of this writing.

---

19   For complete statement please see: Sava WR - 002

ANDREW KOZMA

A MAN, RUNNING

The hall was thirty yards from end to end. The man ran down the hall with determination, without stopping for a breath, heading towards the door waiting there. The door was shut tight. The brass doorknob winked golden in the soft light. The floor was smooth and finished wood, the slats fitting together seamlessly.

He wore jogging pants and a loose running shirt, designed to wick away excess moisture. His dark skin glistened with sweat, but not too much. His shoes were expensive, the kind experienced runners wear marathon after marathon. His stride was long and sure. Without

hurry. And when he reached the end of the hallway, he reached out for the doorknob and winked out of existence with a splash of light.

Slightly before the runner vanished, the runner appeared at the beginning of the hallway, his hand still outstretched, his eyes focused on the doorknob that was now, again, at the other end of the hallway. His eyes downcast, he didn't see himself in the split-second before his other self disappeared.

⧖

"What are we doing with our lives?" Alisa asked.

The runner reached the end of the hallway again, and the automatic counter flipped over another number. The number was in the tens of millions.

"We're pushing the frontiers of scientific exploration," Mitzumi said.

On a sheet he marked the box labeled *No Change*. The paper was lined with boxes, a third of them filled, all of them *No Change*.

Alisa snorted. "We're watching a man run down a hallway, minute after minute, hour after hour, day after day, week after week, month after month."

The cycle started again. Mitzumi marked another box. "You haven't even been here a month."

"Point made," she said. "So, old-timer, has it ever changed?"

"No," Mitzumi confessed, after a moment. He marked another box. "We're making money. That's what we're doing."

"No, I'm getting coffee. That's what *I'm* doing. Want some?"

"You never make it right. More sugar than coffee."

"That's what you get for polluting your coffee to begin with."

Mitzumi marked a number of boxes at once, all *No Change*. They left the observation room, carefully closing the door behind them to hide, at least from casually prying eyes, the fact that they weren't there.

Through the observation glass, the running man reached out for the doorknob but, for a moment, he held back from touching it. For a full second, he hesitated. The other him appeared at the beginning of the hallway, looking down at where the doorknob used to be, as usual. He did not look up to find himself still at the other end of the hall, because by that time the hesitation was over, the other him having vanished like he was always meant to. The second did not see the first, but he was getting closer all the time.

⌛

Alisa's apartment was dark when she returned that night. She sighed in relief. Scott was gone, then, which she couldn't be happier about. Her mother had warned her about seeing her ex before half a year had passed, and, as usual, Alisa ignored her. She hadn't meant to, but Scott knew she'd been having a hard time at work, and had suggested a restaurant she'd always wanted to try.

More importantly, he claimed he just wanted to take her out as a friend.

He was lying, but she didn't care.

In the morning, when she looked at him in the half-light from the dawnlamps, she saw only the innocent boy she'd fallen in love with, the innocent boy who only truly existed when Scott was sleeping. His dark hair mussed, his face unlined except for the scars marking his right cheek. It would be too easy to fall back in.

She left—no note, no goodbye—knowing Scott would understand she didn't want to see him again.

The door sighed open. She kicked off her shoes, dropped her purse, was almost out of her shirt when she noticed someone sitting at the dining table.

Scott.

"Alisa, baby, just listen to me."

His words tumbled out, unbalanced, slurry. He had a wine bottle in his hand, no glass. Finally, she thought, he throws himself into something wholeheartedly.

Alisa roughly tugged her shirt back down, grabbed her shoes and purse, and left. Because she worked at Redux Labs her number went straight through to the police. They sent a patrol to take care of Scott, but she wasn't waiting. They'd get inside, eject him, perhaps arrest him. To be honest, she didn't care anymore. The nightlamps were dim, highlighting the street with shadows. She called Mitzumi, who she knew would still be awake since they'd both just left work.

He didn't answer.

With work taking up so much of her time, Alisa's social life was pretty dismal. She didn't have anyplace else to go.

※

Redux Labs never closed, scientists and assistants and delivery drivers and maintenance people working a twenty-four-hour schedule. The lamps outside the building never swayed from their day setting, so that coming upon the Labs at night always made Alisa think she was approaching a holy city, a halo hugging the entire labyrinthine structure.

But something changed at night. Once the administrators left, half of the building became empty, and that emptiness spread into those parts of Redux Labs that were still occupied. The break room, even though the same number of people were there shirking work, suddenly seemed like the remnants of a party, the popular people having left hours before. The hallways were ghost traps.

Alisa walked through the building uneasily, expecting a security guard to confront her at any moment. And she'd tell them she was here to work—honestly, she had every right to be here now—but she was sure they'd know what had really happened, that she was there simply to avoid an ex, as if all the police and security forces in the world shared the same hive mind.

She passed by her lab, looking through the window to see Taufiq and Leonie, chatting to each other in the same way she and Mitzumi did, killing the boredom one minute at a time. They didn't see her. Over their shoulder, she caught the runner near the end of the hallway, then turned away. Today, tonight, more than ever before, the endless repetition got to her.

There was another woman in the room of cubicles where her desk was located, plugged into headphones and singing out-of-tune. Alisa pulled the chair out from under her desk and scrunched herself in its place, removing the wastebasket's bag to use as a pillow.

⧗

"You're late."

Alisa opened her eyes to Mitzumi sitting in her desk chair.

"I was here before you," she said, her voice rough with sleep.

Mitzumi flicked his eyes to the side, and Alisa focused on the figure she hadn't noticed before. Craig. Their supervisor's supervisor, whom she only ever saw when she was hired. He was not smiling.

"Oh, Craig," Alisa said, putting all of her limited morning professionalism into her voice. "Last night, I stayed extra to work—"

"Don't care," Craig said. He turned to Mitzumi. "We've found your partner. Now let's go."

Out of Craig's field of vision, Mitzumi smiled in apology, but it was a pained smile. Something was wrong. Something big.

Craig turned and vanished out of sight. Mitzumi reached down to help Alisa out, and even though the end result was more awkward than if she'd gotten up herself, she accepted his outstretched hand. After last night's confrontation with Scott, she just wanted some simple, friendly human contact.

"What's going on?" she asked, then noticed that the rest of the room was filled with people at their cubicles, pretending not to stare at the woman who'd been sleeping under her desk. She looked around at them all, forcing an unrepentant smile. "Oh, like you haven't."

Once they were out of the room, Mitzumi's expression darkened.

"He's gone."

⧗

The observation glass was broken, blood streaking what was left. Taufiq was in the runner's hall, face down in a puddle of blood. Glass crunched under her shoes as she walked forward, hands outstretched as though this were all a hologram she could disprove with a touch.

"Where's Leonie?"

"Our clinic," Craig said, his tone making it seem like her being there was Alisa's fault.

She couldn't help getting angry. "And why's Taufiq still there?"

"Because he was dead when security found him. Leonie was not. After the police come and do their thing, we'll take his body out. It's not like the room serves a purpose right now, anyway." Craig turned around to face them. "What happened. Find out."

Even with the observation glass shattered and Taufiq's body on the floor, Alisa still saw the ghost of the runner traveling the hallway. She'd seen him run so many

ANDREW KOZMA　　　　33

times his precise actions were burned into her mind.

"How are we supposed to find out what happened?"

Craig nodded towards Taufiq. "Regarding the runner, you two are the only experts we have remaining. So get to work."

He left, his job clearly done.

There was a familiar smell in the air. Alisa recognized it as blood.

⌛

Alisa and Mitzumi sat in the hallway outside their lab. Mitzumi wrote in a pocket notebook with a wood and silver pen he'd received for his one-year work anniversary. It regularly clogged, so he wiped the tip on his dark pants every few moments to keep the ink running smooth.

"Do we even know the runner's name?"

"I don't." Mitzumi sighed. "I never needed to. I mean, he was right there, running. It would be like learning the name of a lab rat."

"A lab rat's not a person."

Mitzumi shrugged. "Debatable."

"Taufiq's dead, and Leonie's possibly going to die, and you're making jokes?"

"That wasn't a joke. And we can't do anything for them. All we can do is our job."

Alisa kicked the far wall. It made a disappointing thud. "Our *job* was to keep tabs on a man endlessly running down a hallway."

The hallway was empty of other employees, the labs on either side of the hall unused. A wide-shouldered woman turned into the hallway, looked at Alisa and Mitzumi sitting like kids on the floor waiting to be seen by the principal, and went right back the way she'd come. Above them lights flickered and hissed, most of the fluorescents at the end of their life. With the runner gone, their jobs upended, this entire section of Redux Labs seemed obsolete.

"We have to do something," Mitzumi said. Alisa glanced over at his notebook. A numbered list, each number followed by a question mark, sometimes several.

She stood. "You stay here and go through everything in the lab. Maybe there's files or something, I don't know. I'm going to talk with Leonie."

She left before Mitzumi could argue, just like with Scott the night before. The similarity bothered her, as though she were just like the running man, stuck in an endless loop with no definite end and no clear beginning. At the end of the hall, she glanced back. Mitzumi hadn't moved, tapping his pen on the notebook.

⌛

The Redux Labs clinic was located in the highest point of the building, as if the architects believed height equaled health. Perversely, this meant the clinic was the farthest away from the lamps, so that even during the day it was twilight outside, with well-lit landscapes only visible if you walked right up to the windows. It was bright inside, of course, which only made the outside world appear that much darker.

Alisa had no trouble finding Leonie. Police and lab security buzzed around her room, the tension between the two groups palpable. A doctor with short, greasy hair and red-rimmed eyes waved her over.

"You may go right in," he said, clearly relieved she'd arrived.

"Have they already—?" she began to ask the doctor, and though she was sure he heard her—his head twitched at her voice—he didn't stop, didn't turn, simply opened a door marked STAFF ONLY and left.

So Alisa turned to the police, focusing on the closest, who looked like he might be a nice guy out of uniform. His face was boyish behind the professional scowl, his eyes a soft brown.

She gestured to Leonie's room. "Have you already talked with her?"

He pinned her down with his eyes. "They won't let us in until after you talk to her."

"Okay," she said, feeling like she'd shown up for an exam she hadn't studied for. "Well, I'll try to be quick."

"Uh huh," the policeman said, still not looking away. Alisa decided that he wanted her to say something else, something confessional, like his interrogation techniques had bled into every other aspect of his life.

Alisa stepped through the door just as her phone buzzed. A message from Mitzumi. *You've got to see this. Come back as soon as you can.*

Leonie's room was dim. Alisa couldn't see anything, not where the bed was, not whether there was a stool directly in front of her waiting to trip her up, not even if Leonie was, in fact, in the room. Maybe she wasn't that badly hurt and had escaped without anyone noticing. With that crowd outside, that's what Alisa would've done.

"Alisa, is that you?" Leonie asked.

Something was strange about her voice. Not her voice exactly, but the way she spoke. It sounded to Alisa as though Leonie was speaking over herself, her voice doubling.

"Yeah, it's me."

Leonie seemed barely aware that she spoke. With the dim lighting, Alisa could just barely make out the tentacled mass of wires and tubes emerging from her body.

"Turn on the light," she asked, so Alisa flipped the switch, then held her breath to keep from gasping. Leonie was one big bruise, her arms and face swollen so she looked like a blurred picture of herself.

"Turn on the light," Leonie said again.

"I did."

Leonie turned toward Alisa, her eyes somehow simultaneously focused and not focused on her. "You did what?"

"The light. I turned it on."

"Well obviously," Leonie said, the weird doubling in her voice still there, but almost unnoticeable, a split-second echo.

With the light on, Alisa saw something else wrong with Leonie. The light around her shimmered like the air above a hot stove. She reached for a glass of water on the side table, and at the same time she didn't. She grabbed the glass, drank in tiny, desperate gulps, and returned the glass to the table. But a glass remained in the hand she brought back to rest on her chest.

Alisa wanted to take some notes. She wanted to film this, to record it, to be behind tempered observation glass. But she didn't know if Leonie knew what was going on, and she didn't want to startle her. Yet Alisa couldn't stop staring at the two glasses of water. Whatever had happened to Leonie, it was contagious.

"Do you remember what happened?" she asked, managing to keep her voice calm.

"He went crazy," Leonie said, her voice coming into perfect alignment with itself, her body settling down, everything about her normal and singular. Except for the water glass. "One moment Taufiq and me were joking around, the next, we looked up and he was there at the glass. He's not even supposed to be able to see us! You know that."

"I know."

"He punched through it. Punched through it! That stuff is bulletproof." She trailed off,

and though her lips were closed, Alisa heard her say, "I don't believe it."

"I don't believe it either."

Leonie squinted her eyes at Alisa. "Alisa, I need to ask you a favor. We don't know each other for shit, and you know I wouldn't ask anything if I didn't have to, but—"

At the same time, another Leonie moved out-of-sync with the first, both of them together looking like heads of a hydra. This one said, her eyes wide with fear, "Look, I need to tell you something, and I know, god I know, you have no reason to believe me, but—"

After that, the voices were smashed together, incomprehensible. Alisa wasn't sure, but there might've been more than two voices there. Three, four, maybe. With each word another voice appeared until her ears were full of a single, undistinguished buzz in the key of Leonie. Alisa backed away, reaching out behind her until her outstretched fingers jammed themselves against the door. The noise of voices was a tide pushing her back, battering against her skull.

She knew what it must look like to Leonie, her co-worker suddenly horrified at something you've said. Scared. Disgusted.

A water glass smashed against the wall, barely missing Alisa. A water glass was still in her hand. On the side table next to Leonie's bed. An infinite supply of water glasses.

A MAN, RUNNING

Alisa backed through the door, telling Leonie, "I know, I know, I'll do what I can," not knowing at all.

In the hall outside, the police and lab security looked at her deadpan. With the door closed, it sounded like Leonie was having a very loud, very involved conversation with herself. Another glass shattered.

Alisa walked away. A man's voice called after her, "What did you find out?"

"Don't let her touch you."

Mitzumi sat cross-legged in the middle of the lab on the hard floor surrounded by cardboard storage boxes, open file folders, faded documents, photocopied photographs.

"You won't believe it," he said as Alisa entered.

Alisa glanced at Taufiq's dead body in the observation hall, still in the same place it was before. "There's very little I wouldn't believe right now."

"Ha. Ha ha." Mitzumi took a file from a box and threw it at his computer terminal. "None of this is on the servers. None of it. And it's exactly what we're studying!"

Alisa couldn't focus. She heard Leonie's frightened voices in her ears, insistent and pleading. And when she looked at Taufiq's body, she felt just like Leonie. Frightened of what was happening. Insistent that it shouldn't be happening. Pleading with someone, anyone, to let this be a dream. But Taufiq didn't disappear, the glass didn't re-collect itself into an unbroken sheet. The running man wasn't back running his pointless Möbius lap.

"Don't you get it?" Mitzumi said, his voice breaking. "The answers we've been looking for, they were already here!"

"When I first started, you said we weren't looking for anything. And from all we've done, I mean, come on, Mitzumi. We make sure everything's working and that the lab rat hasn't died."

"The lab rat," he says, sliding a photograph across the floor towards her.

The black-and-white photo looked like it was from an ID, just the head and a bit of starch-collared shirt. In it, the running man was smiling nervously, as though convinced he had a bit of lettuce between his teeth. At the top of the photo was a name. Joseph Millar. At the bottom was a faded date.

"Is that date correct?"

"What date?"

"The picture's from twenty years ago." She handed the photo to Mitzumi. "He doesn't look any different."

Which wasn't exactly true. The running man wore lightweight pants and a wicking shirt, his short hair shiny with sweat, his determined expression clean of any fear or nervousness. But it was the same guy, not having aged at all.

She glanced back towards the bland hallway Joseph Millar had spent the last twenty years running down. It didn't seem possible. It definitely wasn't logical.

"What was the point?" she murmured.

"That's what you won't believe." Mitzumi answered her. "This was a power plant."

"A power plant?" Alisa echoed.

She saw movement out of the corner of her eye and turned to where Taufiq's body lay. Was the body where it had been all this time, or had it slid closer to the broken window?

Of course, any movement she thought she noticed was just a trick of the eye, her nerves rattled by whatever it was she'd seen up in Leonie's room. Mitzumi shoved three boxes towards her, the cardboard rasping against the polished concrete floor.

"That," he nodded towards the observation hall, "is the power plant. These boxes have all the details. Apparently, I mean I've only skimmed, but apparently it gets power by using the body of..." he paused. "The running man."

"Joseph Millar."

Mitzumi made a pained face. "Yeah. Sure. The running man."

The boxes before Alisa took on a forbidding aspect. "What do you mean the power plant uses his body? Is that some sort of hamster wheel out there?"

Mitzumi laughed. He looked excited by what he'd figured out, the truth behind what they'd been doing, all of it making sense now. She thought about how she didn't really know him at all. Just like she didn't know Scott, and what he might be capable of.

"Every time the running man reaches the end of the hall and tries to touch the doorknob, he completes a circuit sending him back to the beginning of the hall," Mitzumi said, his voice full of wonder. "But there was a side effect. When he gets sent back, there's a double of him created at the same time."

     A MAN, RUNNING

Alisa couldn't stand the excitement in his voice. She looked at Taufiq's body, the end result of this process that's been going on for twenty years. It had moved again, now slightly farther away. Underneath it was an old bloodstain, faded and worn into the floor. But she also saw brighter blood reflecting the light from the lab itself.

"Don't you want to understand?" Mitzumi asked, frustrated at her lack of interest. "You're a scientist. This is *science*."

She answered just to satisfy him. "Sure. So what happened?"

"They thought they'd invented time travel. And maybe they had. But somehow the running man—"

"Millar," she said.

"Sure. He appeared back in time slightly before himself. It wasn't time travel, but a merging of alternate dimensions. Or an incomplete splitting of realities. And in order to deal with this constant multiplication, they decided to use those copied bodies as fuel."

Mitzumi rattled a sheaf of pages as though the words and formulas typed there explained the universe. Maybe they did. Alisa was out of her depth here. Hell, she never even finished her dissertation. Her job at Redux only required she be working towards finishing it, which in her mind meant never.

"After each copy is created, it's sucked from the observation room and fed into the power plant."

"They're killed?" Alisa asked.

Mitzumi laughed. "That's the beauty of it! They weren't ever really alive to begin with."

Something was wrong with his laughter. Is that what hysteria sounded like? An overdose of earnestness?

Alisa needed to sit down, but she didn't want to touch this room any more than she had to. The whole place felt radioactive, as if even a month's exposure of working here had poisoned her body beyond repair.

"We were killing him." Her stomach roiled. "That's what we were doing here."

"Not at all. We were just here to make sure nothing went wrong."

Now it was Alisa's turn to laugh. "Well good on us, then, for not fucking up."

For the first time since she'd entered the room, Mitzumi's mood darkened. Petulantly, he nodded towards Taufiq's body. "It wasn't us who fucked up."

Alisa rubbed her eyes until lights flashed against the black of her eyelids. "So have you discovered *anything* useful?"

"Have you?" he retorted.

"Leonie's out of joint, time-wise. There are multiples of her at the same time, in the same space."

"The running man must've touched her."

Alisa nodded. "Whatever he has, it's contagious."

"That's not possible."

"Fine, it's not possible," she said. "What about Millar?"

"Security is sure he couldn't possibly have gotten out of the labs. But if he did, after all that time in the hallway, I mean, there's been no studies about what that kind of spatial distortion would do to a person. He's probably insane."

Alisa took in everything in the running man's hallway, how it was designed to look like a common corridor in someone's house, fake-wood paneling on the walls, worn actual-wood floors, the doorknobs with the push-button locks that wouldn't stop a determined toddler. Darker squares on the wall seemed to indicate where pictures once hung. A perfectly recreated hallway.

Except for Taufiq's dead body. Except for the one-way observation glass. Except that no one lived in that hallway, in that fake house. Except for Joseph Millar, who'd been running for at least twenty years, never getting anywhere, leaving nothing behind him except enough fuel to power a city.

"Where did he live?" Mitzumi rattled off an address. An hour walk, maybe. If she took a cab, she could get there in no time. Mitzumi groaned. "What is it?"

"What is what?" he asked.

On the other side of the observation window, Taufiq's body moved. His body lay in his dried blood. His body also twitched, an arm lifting up, a hand pushing down, collapsing in exhaustion.

"Taufiq," she whispered.

Mitzumi stepped up beside her. Both of them stared together as Taufiq simultaneously lay there, dead as dead can be, and tried to crawl towards them.

"Help me," the not-dead Taufiq said, slowly crawling out of his dead self, inching closer and closer to the broken window.

"Whatever you do, don't let him touch you," Alisa said, already out the door.

In the cab on the way to Millar's address, Alisa saw a number of strange things. A couple arguing with themselves. A full trashcan both upright and turned over, and a young girl picking up the spilled trash and piling it onto the full trashcan. A series of calico cats chasing their own tail. She kept her window shut, as if a pane of glass could insulate her from whatever Millar was bringing into the world.

Before leaving Redux Labs, she'd called Craig to report in. He'd sounded harried, overworked, and had just told her to "Deal with it, okay, we've got enough problems as it is."

Then she'd dialed the number for lab security, but all she got was a recorded message, meaning either their phone lines were all taken up with other calls or their message inbox was full. Or both.

But Craig and security, they'd only be handling the symptoms. Millar was the problem, and so Alisa went to find him, even though she had no idea what she'd do when she found him. The cab driver didn't seem phased by any of the things Alisa saw, but then again maybe the woman just didn't notice, maybe she sees enough in her workday to callous her to the odd and strange unless the odd and strange gets in the cab to ask for a ride.

As they drove the daylamps flickered. Not all of them, and not all at once, but the cab driver noticed.

"Did you see that?" she asked, answering herself as if she never expected fares to talk to her. "The daylamps wizzed out for a second. Never seen that before."

But the flickering chilled Alisa through and through, because she couldn't help wondering how much power Millar's copies had provided. Would the city collapse entirely without Millar running down that hallway?

Alisa had the cab driver let her off at the intersection closest to Millar's apartment building. A homeless man walking down the other side of the street had an octopus's worth of arms. The cab driver sped up as soon as she passed him, pulling around the corner with a squeal of tires.

The neighborhood was in disrepair. Full trash bags littered the sidewalk next to full trashcans. The apartment building Millar had lived in was five stories tall, made entirely of brown bricks, covered in stains from mold and moisture. Lights were on behind some of the windows, but just as many were broken. Maybe twenty

years ago it was in better shape, but it was hard to imagine this place ever as new. The name, written across the front entrance, was The Savoy.

There was no doorman and the door was unlocked. The entrance hall was lit with a few bare bulbs. There was a tiny guard station next to the ensconced metal mailboxes, but no guard. The marble floor was cracked, the cracks filled with dirt. The tiniest weeds grew from the dirt. Alisa wanted to replant them outside, where at least the light would be better.

It was obvious Millar had been here. Footsteps shimmered on the floor, bits of marble that were dirty one moment, then dirtier the next, the muck of time doubled in only those places.

Millar's old address was on the second floor. Alisa walked across the marble slowly, carefully avoiding Millar's trail. She didn't want to do this. This wasn't really her job. The lights in the building went out for a moment, then came back overly bright before settling into a shuddery dimness.

Alisa's phone buzzed twice in quick succession. A message from her mom, saying that even though she was disappointed Alisa and Scott were back together, it wasn't right of Alisa to treat him so badly, so she'd given him the spare key to Alisa's apartment that was only supposed to be used for emergencies.

Which meant Alisa wasn't going home anytime soon.

The second message was from Mitzumi. *Leonie's dead.*

Chills ran up her spine. Except for the time-out-of-joint effects, Leonie had been fine when Alisa'd seen her. Did security kill her once they saw she was infectious? She didn't think that would make sense for Redux, but then again she wasn't sure they knew what they were doing. They hadn't understood what was happening with Millar, just used the inexplicable result as an energy resource. They were flying just as blind as she was.

"You're from Redux, aren't you?" a man asked. She looked up to find Joseph Millar on the stairs, at most fifteen feet away. Alisa expected there to be a shimmer around him, just like with the people and things he'd touched, but he looked like the same man she'd seen every day for the past month, only this time not running.

"Yeah, I am," Alisa said.

Millar sat down on the lowest step. Exhaustion was in every line of his face, the way his body sagged even as he leaned against the wall. He opened his mouth to say something, then looked away. At first Alisa thought it was sweat. Tears collected in his eyes, but he wiped them away before they fell.

"I didn't realize how much time had passed." His voice was a smooth tenor. Watching him in the lab, Alisa had imagined it deeper, almost angry. "Twenty years, right?"

She nodded. "Twenty years."

Millar wiped his eyes again, then his nose. "Do you know where my wife and kids are?"

She shook her head.

"Are they dead?"

"I don't know."

The longer Millar sat there, the more shimmery the steps around him became. They gained a sort of visual weight, as though more of the stair was there, more and more of the same thing in the same space, the cheap stone and metal treads increasingly themselves. He leaned back completely against the stairs, stared up at the ceiling.

"I'm sorry about those two at the lab," he said. "I didn't know what was happening at first, you know. I saw myself up ahead at the door, touching the door knob, and disappearing, and it was like I woke from a dream. I knew where I was, that the hallway's right wall was actually a window, and I broke it. And when they tried to stop me, I just shoved them out of the way. The man flew back like a baseball."

Millar gripped the edge of one step in frustration, the stone pressing out between his fingers like putty.

"There's something wrong with me. I know. All I wanted was to see them again."

He stood up shakily, like he was drunk, or starving, or so exhausted he might sleep right there where he was standing, consciousness going out like a light.

"Are you okay?" Alisa asked. She couldn't think of what else to say.

"It seemed like thirty minutes I was in there. And I'm not any older, am I? I'm not any older." He looked down at his body, as though the answers were buried in his clothing, his flesh. "But everyone else is."

The lights dimmed, went out for a long moment, then came back to the same dimness. Alisa jumped back. Millar was right in front of her.

"Thank you for coming to look for me." He didn't sound thankful. "Don't do it again."

Millar pushed the front door open and left. For a second, the door remained closed as he walked through it. Alisa found another exit.

⧗

The guards at Redux Labs waved Alisa on through while they nervously scanned the streets. The lights around the Labs were the only ones lit for a good distance, most of the daylamps off or so dim as to be useless. The hallways were empty. A few people huddled in their cubicles.

Alisa passed a conference room filled with a dozen scientists furiously arguing. She imagined everyone else had abandoned the building as the crisis became real, going home to their families or to hide in bars, wherever they felt the most safe, but Alisa didn't have that choice.

Scott was in her home, clearly not going anywhere. Her mom was so deluded about her life that they might as well be strangers. Her job at Redux had been her last real chance to make a life for herself, to create that career she dreamed of all throughout college and grad school, and instead she'd been a glorified camera, a visual stenographer.

She couldn't stop thinking about how Millar had been so lost, a man out of time, barely aware how much time had passed. What must the world have looked like on his way out of the lab, through the city, to the place where, in his mind, he'd lived just a few hours before? Alisa couldn't imagine.

But it was seductive. Not that sense of loss, but the idea of stepping away from her life for a half hour and coming back to something completely new, utterly different, a world she could make herself new in.

The lab was unguarded. Mitzumi was gone, as was Taufiq's body, though the blood remained on the floor. She climbed through the broken window, cutting her hand on the glass, leaving drops of her blood to join Taufiq's. She stood at one end of the hallway. The brass knob of the far door was as shiny as it had ever been, untouched by Millar.

Alisa wiped her bleeding hand on her pants, then began to walk, easing into a gentle run. Her footsteps were loud in the hall, pounding like an extra heartbeat.

ANDREW KOZMA

The door came closer and closer until she knew this was it, there was no going back. She ran and she reached out. She reached out and she ran.

A MAN, RUNNING

HENRY SANDERS-WRIGHT

THERE'S NO-ONE LEFT TO HAUNT

The first rays of the morning sun peek through the blinds of my small flat, lighting my living room in blades of gloomy gray. With a shudder, the black, rotting flesh of my old face groans to life. It turns away from the wall that it's been staring at dead-eyed all night. Halfway through its shuffling pivot, it locks eyes with me. The expression doesn't change, but I know what's going on in its decrepit little mind.

It's remembering that I'm not food.

I roll my eyes. "Hurry up or you'll miss the herd."

I'm never sure if it understands me, but my zombified corpse responds with a moan and crosses our small flat to the door. Wait—is it missing an ear? How long has that been gone?

Death is shit, Holly. If you're dead, I hope you were spared this, because I hate being a ghost. If you're still alive, then don't die.

I look at the pictures on the wall, the same my corpse stares at nightly. Moments from your childhood, smiling back at me from behind long dark hair. I'm sure I was there when a few of those were taken, but it's probably not as many as I think. I wish I could take one with me—something to keep you close. But, annoyingly, ghost pockets don't work. Nothing does when you're incorporeal. I'm a dimly glowing breeze now.

Dead or alive, I hope you're doing better than I am.

A tugging pulls gently at my chest, beckoning me towards the front door. Death is particularly shit when you're anchored to your own decomposing corpse, like an ethereal balloon tied to a profoundly ugly and deeply stupid dog.

"Are you getting faster or am I getting slower?" I call after it, but it doesn't respond.

I get up from my once-cream sofa, where I've spent the night waiting for dawn, and stretch, relishing in it. There's no physical relief for my phantom body—it just feels right. It's the only part of my morning routine I can still do.

I take another look at the pictures of you, each artfully folded to crop out your mum. "See you later, kiddo."

The ethereal leash pulls on me harder, threatening to drag me along as my corpse descends the stairs. "I'm coming!"

I follow my remains out, passing the mound of dirty laundry that's been festering in the corner for six months. In life, it never bothered me if it was left for a week or two. Death has pushed many of my limits. I've never wanted to do the laundry more.

Stepping over the wreck of my front door, bashed down by my zombie on our first night together, I catch up with my corpse downstairs before it joins the herd. It's rush hour as the building's undead file out into the street, a few followed by ghosts of other unlucky tenants. They look as miserable as I feel.

Catching eyes with my remaining neighbours, we exchange brief nods. As was the case in life, we have nothing to talk about.

We join the zombie herd, glowing fish in an ocean of the undead, swept along by the tide towards the city. Everyday, the zombies come and go—to work and to home—spurred on by muscle memory, something etched deep within their decaying minds. A never-ending Monday.

Between the sea of decaying faces and ragged breaths frosting like cursed sea foam, I glimpse other ghosts, easily noticeable by the downcast eyes and lack of burrowing maggots. None of us have any choice in this cyclical hell—we're all along for the ride.

I don't really mind the commute. It's probably what's kept me sane. The nights are long and boring, and I can't sleep anymore. I'm stuck at home in the dark with only my rotting corpse for company. Out here, at least I'm moving, going somewhere, doing something.

An hour into the march—or possibly two, I don't know, I didn't die wearing a watch—I look up from my shuffling feet.

The buildings on either side of the street have grown taller and wider, blending from brick to steel as we cross from suburbia into the city centre. The damage is worse here: burnt cars gridlocked for eternity, blown out shop windows like gaping pores, and glass ground daily into a fine sand by thousands of feet. The city has a hangover it will never recover from.

Shouting rolls across the top of the herd. The undead don't notice, so I know it's another ghost. Unless it's their own spirit, zombies can't see or hear ghosts. Even if the zombies could see us, they wouldn't care. They can't eat us. As soon as mine realised that, I was dead to him.

"Not here! You couldn't have made it a bit further, you lazy bastard?"

I spot the source of the shouting—a man caught in the middle of the herd's flow. Zombies pass through him, completely unaware. He shudders when they do, growing angrier each time. I'm almost jealous. I haven't been that angry in months.

"Mind where you're going, you rotting assholes!"

Curious and almost excited for a change of pace, I drift closer. A mound of dirty sludge is heaped at his feet, crawling with flies. Bones poke from the pile. I wince, knowing exactly what it is.

Our eyes meet, and he calms. He's clean-shaven, wearing a tailored suit, hair freshly cut and groomed—at least, it was six months ago. I hope he was happy with the haircut, because it's like that for eternity now. I wouldn't be.

"I thought I had longer," he says, anger melting away. His eyes drop to the mound, what had recently been his zombie and, before that, him. Now it's just an anchor, tying him to the middle of the street for who knows how long. Probably forever.

What do you say to someone like that, Holly?

Tentatively, I open my mouth to offer empty condolences, but a powerful and unpleasant shiver interrupts me. My corpse steps through me, the rotting sludge, the man, and then continues on. It never breaks its pace.

"You utter prick," I mutter at my own back.

The man looks between my corpse and I, realisation bubbling into an anger more violent than before as he sees the lingering similarity between us. Quickly and awkwardly, I follow the dirty footprints of my zombie. The man screams curses after me as I leave.

Even when the shouting is far behind, I can't shake the thought of the man. He's a reminder of the inevitable. My corpse is doomed for the same fate. They all are. Flesh isn't made to last. Axes, guns and tanks are like sharpened sticks compared to the best zombie-killer: time.

Great news for anyone still living, bad news for the new ghost community. Anchored to our remains, we won't be able to go farther than thirty feet in any direction.

Stuck here.

Forever.

I don't let my corpse leave my sight for the rest of the commute. Usually, I can't stand looking at it—a reminder of what I was. Now I'm fascinated by it, analysing every inch, trying to work out how many commutes it has left.

It's definitely slower than the others, its paces shorter. More flies too, although I'm not confident what that means. It probably reeks.

More... *bits* have been falling off it lately, although I'd thought it was more due to ineptitude than rot. Its biggest threat is itself. It's never even bit anyone. Should I be relieved or disappointed by that?

I made a poor zombie, Holly. I'm sure you know I wasn't exactly a great human, either, but I didn't think I'd make for such a dreadful zombie.

My corpse shambles onward to my office, ambivalent to my analysis and most of the world around it. I flinch when another zombie bumps shoulders with it. The realisation comes to me then as it teeters, barely managing to stay upright.

It's not going to last much longer, is it?

"Fuck."

I shiver, feeling the chains tying me to the earth tighten. I don't have long.

Being a ghost didn't come with a guide or rulebook. Horror movies were only ten percent accurate. When we died in the rising, everyone left a zombie behind, but not everyone left a ghost. The vast majority of people fucked off to whatever pearly gates are beyond this existence, leaving their corpse behind like a snake shedding skin.

According to the supernatural grapevine, unfinished business holds the rest of us back. Tasks on Earth we have to complete before we're free. We weren't given a lot of time to tie up loose ends when the dead rose. Honestly, it's surprising that more people weren't held back.

In contemporary times, the norm was to haunt a house for a century or two and bother a family until they got so sick of you that they went out of their way to get rid of you.

Now there's nobody left to haunt.

I want to finish my business, but I don't know what I'm meant to do. Incorporeality doesn't help, either, and the only tool at my disposal is falling apart, braindead and as useful as a ghost's toothbrush. Still, it's better than nothing. Through excessive motioning and a lot of shouting, I've baited and manipulated my zombie into achieving simple tasks. It has led to some creative problem solving.

I died on my lunch break, so at first I figured if I made my corpse attend all the meetings I had scheduled for that after-noon, that would sort it. It was easy: my corpse still hadn't yet grasped the concept that it couldn't eat me, so it followed me obediently from room to room, biting me constantly. Unpleasant, but efficient.

I've also tried tidying my desk (lacking any coordination, my corpse only made things worse), feeding the office cat (ending with my corpse herding it into a group of zombies—R.I.P. Tallulah) and clearing out my email inbox. That last one took some real patience, as I tried to get my corpse to hit various keys through shouting and pointing. My laptop died just before we got into my emails. I've never felt such anguish.

Unsure what else I could do, I stopped trying months ago. I still don't know.

You would though. God, I wish you were here.

I have to do it today, before it's too late. There must be something. I don't want to end up like the man in the suit, alone and stuck between two places until the end of time.

My corpse and I slowly peel away from the herd as zombies disperse into various offices, shops and restaurants. We pass the local Pret and I avoid looking at it. Bad service, cold coffee, and being killed with nothing but a "Wiltshire-cured ham & greve cheese baguette" to defend yourself really changes your perception of a place.

We make it to the office: a squat, five floor concrete building squeezed between towers twice its height. I'm not sure what has saved it from refurbishment. It's a bit of an eyesore, but part of me does have a soft spot for its outdated, bleak design.

As my corpse shuffles over, I search by the office doors. My unfinished business probably isn't outside, but I'm not taking any chances. Maybe I'm supposed to clean up the cigarette ends that litter the smokers' area? Surely not. I only ever smoked at business lunches with clients.

My zombie doesn't even glance at me as it steps through the closed automatic doors, the glass smashed during the rising. I hope my fate doesn't lie in the cigarette butts as the leash between us drags me inside.

As with every day, I follow my corpse as it repeats my daily work routine. It seems to knock into every colleague and wall in its path, and I find myself wincing with each one. In truth, I wouldn't mind it stopping here. Better than the road, and the office always felt like home to me. Probably why your Mum hated the place—and me, for that matter.

First, my corpse takes us to the coffee machine to stand with a few other zombies for ten minutes. Zombie gossip is mostly silent, occasionally punctuated by a groan. Ghost gossip isn't much better. Despite a number of my colleagues' corpses milling around, only a few have their spirits still attached. A lot of my colleagues were more ready to die than I gave them credit for.

I use the time to search the break area, looking under the small white tables and colourful plastic chairs. Maybe I didn't clean away after myself? I hope it's not that. The contents of the bins have been spread to the four corners of the room and I'm not confident I could get my zombie to clean it if I had eternity.

My remaining incorporeal colleagues give me questioning looks, but say nothing. Another benefit to death: we don't have to pretend we like each other anymore.

Done with its chit-chat, my corpse takes us on a slow journey up three flights of stairs to my desk, where it will stand for the next eight hours. The climb is particularly agonising to watch today, so I go ahead and wait by my desk as soon as I have enough slack on my leash.

A picture of you is blu-tacked to my monitor. You're older than you are on the walls at home, dressed as the Wicked Witch for a school play. I smile when I see it, but only now do I wish I had seen the play. At least my corpse hasn't knocked the picture off with everything else.

The sun is shining through the office window, high and bright in the sky by now. I look up and squint through the sunlight, but I don't feel its warmth.

I hope you don't have to suffer this.

I look at the chaotic mess that had once been my desk, trying to spot *anything* I've overlooked. By the time my corpse finally arrives, I'm pacing the room anxiously. I have no leads and my zombie took longer than usual to arrive.

"Don't you dare stop on the stairs. I'm not spending eternity between the second and third floors."

My corpse ignores me as it stumbles in front of the desk. While it stands there, slack-jawed, staring at the monitor in what I'm sure is some form of undead mockery, I explore the length of my leash, walking back and forth across the office. Every lap of the floor gets faster as I cross possibilities out in my head, stamping back and forth, knowing I'd done this all before months ago.

When I return to my desk, my zombie taunts me with a blank look. *Buckle up for eternity, pal.* I scream. My fists passes through its face as I try to punch it. All I get is a buzzing shiver up my arm.

Surprised by my sudden attack, my corpse falls backwards onto my desk, smacking the monitor onto the floor. The picture of you is trapped beneath.

For a moment, I worry my zombie isn't getting up, but it manages to right itself. It looks at me, almost expectantly.

"Sorry. You didn't deserve that," I say.

It groans at me, which could mean anything, but I like to think it's accepted my apology. Teetering into movement, my corpse knocks against my desk and towards the door. I wonder where he's off to until I see others ambling the same way. Lunchtime. That's the fastest a morning has gone in six months.

I'm about to follow when something catches my eye. From the gap behind where my monitor stood, a red folder flops onto my desk. I don't remember that? It must have been wedged back there. Probably misplaced by Julian. The man was so scatterbrained in life, I'm surprised the zombies didn't ignore him.

The tugging starts—my corpse must be faster going down the stairs than going up. I follow, slowly. Lunchtime is my second most disliked part of the day, after the entirety of the night. If I listed it all out, there's probably only a very narrow part of the day I can actually stand.

There's a line at the Pret by the time I catch up. Corpses politely queuing still surprises me, a habit even death can't break. Inside, a few ghosts are sat at tables, eyes closed, likely imagining themselves anywhere but here. They look like they're having the time of their undead lives.

I wait outside for my zombie to shuffle up to the counter, stare silently at the cashier for a few minutes, then leave. I can't go inside, not after how things ended. The fact that I'm brought back here every day is the biggest joke of my death. Imagine being haunted by a sandwich shop.

The idea of my corpse collapsing here crosses my mind. I zombie-watch to distract myself. How many of them did I know? Most are too rotted—you definitely wouldn't recognise mine. A rare few even have makeshift weapons lodged in them, like a fork in the eye or a pen sprouting from the forehead. Speaking of Julian, I'm sure I saw him in the early days with a laptop charger wrapped around his—

Oh.

The red file—it's not Julian's, it's my quarterly report. Sat on my desk since the start of the uprising, it was due the day of my death. It's about two quarters late.

"Oh shit."

That's it! My unfinished business! I'm sure of it.

I peer through the shop window and spot my zombie at the front of the queue. "Hurry up!"

Ghosts frown at me, wondering what I have to be urgent about. I ignore them.

This is it. I have my way out.

My zombie ambles out, ignoring my urging as it makes its steady way back to the office. It seems even slower than before. I rush ahead of it as far as I can, the leash trying to pull me back. I struggle against it, desperate to get back to my desk.

As soon as my corpse is close enough, I go back and stare at the red folder. I can't believe I'd forgotten about it. It took me three weeks to put it together. One busy lunchtime managed to completely wipe it from my mind.

When my corpse arrives, I wave and click in front of its face to get its attention.

It takes a lot of movement, but it finally responds with a low moan, looking at me with milky eyes.

"Pick this up!" I point frantically at the folder on the desk.

My corpse stares at me blankly.

"Pick it up!" I scoop at the folder like an overly-aggressive mime. My hands pass through it, tickling unpleasantly, but I repeat it, hoping something will get through to my zombie.

After a frustratingly long few minutes, my corpse moves forward and claws at the desk. It looks more like it's digging than trying to pick something up, but I don't care. As long as it does what I need, that's all that matters.

Clumsily, it manages to scrabble the folder into its arms. I cheer and my zombie almost drops the folder in surprise. I pray my paper-clipping skills are enough to hold the folder together.

"Come on! There's a tasty person over here. All helpless and ready to be eaten." I run ahead of it as far as I can before the leash between us strains, trying to pull me back. The tether goes slack as my corpse gets the idea and follows, shambling after me.

I lead it through the maze of desks to the other side of the third floor where my manager's office is. Caution hasn't completely abandoned me. I choose the widest paths between the desks, trying to minimise the risk of a fall my corpse wouldn't get up from. Death won't have the last laugh—not this time.

Waiting for my corpse by the open office door, I'm bouncing from foot to foot. I can't remember the last time I was this excited, even before death.

As my corpse catches up, I step into the office. My manager's zombie stands behind a desk, wearing a once-pink shirt, and greets my corpse with a groan that passes right through me. I'm surprised that my manager wasn't kept behind. He was cheating on his husband and everyone knew about his coke addiction. If anyone had something unfinished, it should have been him.

"Here's that report you wanted," I say to my manager's bloated corpse, excitedly. Probably too much, especially as it can't hear or see me.

I motion to my corpse to put the folder on the desk. It stares back. I sigh and throw my arms in front of me several times. It mimics me and the report flops unceremoniously onto the desk between us.

The remains of my manager grunts at the report, then turns away.

That's it. It's done. There is absolutely nothing left more for me to do. I need fireworks to be going off right now, along with a round of applause and a final pint of Stella.

My business on Earth is finished.

How will it come? Angelic light? Hellfire? Will it be painful?

     THERE'S NO-ONE LEFT TO HAUNT

I look around for a sign. Nothing. I look down at my hands, hoping it will be a simple and undramatic fading from existence. I really hope it doesn't hurt.

My zombie watches me - can it see it happening? At least this will be the last time I'll have to look at my own rotting face. I blow it a kiss.

My corpse quickly loses interest in me and shambles away. I don't follow it until the chain starts to tow me along, forcing me to close the distance. Even then, I don't join it back at my desk. I stop at the far end of the tether between the second and third floor, staring at the speckled floor tiles.

I don't understand. The report *has* to be my unfinished business. My life was spent in this office and I've scoured it. There's nothing left for me to do. Nothing to hand over to my shoddy replacement. Why can't I leave?

Maybe it was all bollocks. I've never actually seen any other spirits leave this miserable existence. For all I know, it could be ghostly rumor, a vain hope of escape. I believed it, easily. It was a light to stay on in the dark. Eternity doesn't seem so long when you don't think it's forever.

But maybe that's part of the punishment. Stringing us along, making us think we can escape, stretching years into centuries into millennia until the end of time. I see it now. You can't torture someone that's given up. Bravo to Satan for that master stroke.

I punch the wall, but my hand passes through, sending that uncomfortable buzz up my arm. I don't remove my arm immediately. It's not painful, just annoying, but it's something. If this was a punishment, wouldn't it have pain?

I don't know what this is anymore. I just want to leave. I want it all to end.

I wish you were here, Holly. Even if you couldn't help me. I know I don't deserve it, but seeing you again would make my afterlife.

Figures stumble through me, along with my own corpse, and I realise how much time has passed. Home time. I leave the office, probably for the last time, and join my undead colleagues in the dying light. Surprisingly, part of me is relieved. I don't want to spend eternity in the office. Your mum wouldn't believe me if she heard that.

Trailing behind my corpse, I stare at my own feet. The last thing I need is to watch my zombie nearly topple for the entire journey. The anticipation is the worst. At least the first time I died it was over before you could say "Pret A Manger." Getting my guts ripped open wasn't even that bad in hindsight. I'd prefer it again over the eternity I'm about to face.

HENRY SANDERS-WRIGHT

The walk home feels longer than usual, as if my despair is weighing my corpse down too. We flag behind and the herd eventually moves on without us. By the time we reach our apartment building, it's almost pitch black. A thin veneer of moonlight only serves to give the bones of the old world a faint outline. It's enough to find my way in.

I'm surprised my zombie can still manage the stairs, but it tackles them, one shaky step at a time.

Surely it can't go much further. If there's any mercy left in the world, it'll collapse in my living room. I think I can deal with haunting the flat for eternity. At least I can see you until the pictures fade. And I know no-one will touch my stuff. I'd even be okay with the stairs.

Anywhere but the road. Existence would be marked by the passing of the herd twice a day until it marches itself to dust, and then it would be a long nothing. Knowing my luck, I'd be stuck next to the man from this morning.

I reach our floor, relief washing through me. My corpse has stopped a few metres from the front door. It tilts its head from side to side. I frown. Is this it? I suppose the hallway is close enough.

My corpse sniffs at the air, once, then twice. Faster than I expected, it stumbles over the wreck of the front door and disappears inside.

"What's got you so excited?"

I follow but stop short when I hear a grunt, a thwack and a heavy thud.

Someone is here. Someone alive.

And they've just killed my zombie.

I enter the flat, cautiously peering around the corner. Old instincts, even after all this time. I have nothing to fear. I can't die a third time.

The stark light of a torch highlights my corpse flat on its back, unmoving. An axe splattered with gore has split the top of its skull. An unexpected tightness forms in my chest when I see my dead zombie. I'm going to miss the conversation.

My eyes follow the torch beam to face the killer, mulling over whether to thank or curse them. "Holy shit."

It's you.

You're here!

"Oh fuck," you say as you bend down to inspect my corpse. "Sorry about that, Dad."

I forget myself and step over my corpse to hug you. My arms slip through you like smoke. You shiver and tense, looking around warily, but you're alone.

"You look well, Holly. Better than me." I study your face in the torchlight. You look thinner, definitely a lot grimier, but you've survived well.

It makes me proud to say that you look badass. Your long dark hair is short and jagged—who cut it? A blind guy with a shard of glass? It's less fashionable for

     THERE'S NO-ONE LEFT TO HAUNT

sure, but I suppose more convenient. Zombies aren't going to be yanking it back for a bite.

You always were smart.

You wrench the ax free, throwing skull shards and brains everywhere. "I can never fail to give you a headache."

You always were a bit of a smart arse too. We know where you get that from.

"I wanted to see you both. I looked for Mum first but I couldn't find her. Maybe she's still out there," you tell my corpse, your voice low. I hope your mother is suffering as much as I am. "I'm surprised you're here—I thought you would be at the office, even after hours."

There's a stinging edge to your voice that hurts, even though it's well-deserved. Six months ago, I would have argued back, telling you I work hard for us— for you. I've had a lot of time to think in six months.

"I knew you'd be a zombie."

What's that supposed to mean?

"I almost didn't come," you say. "But I needed to know what happened to you, so I'm not left wondering. I don't like leaving anything unfinished—even if it is to your zombie."

I smile. *My clever girl.*

Quiet stretches between us. There's something absolute about the quiet and then I realise it's the first time in six months I haven't had to listen to my zombie's ragged breath. Already, I find myself enjoying it.

Maybe some actual peace and quiet for eternity won't be so bad.

You run a hand through your hair, blowing out air slowly as if releasing a pressure inside.

I miss when your hair was longer. You look too grown-up now. It reminds me of what I've missed.

"You were a shit, Dad."

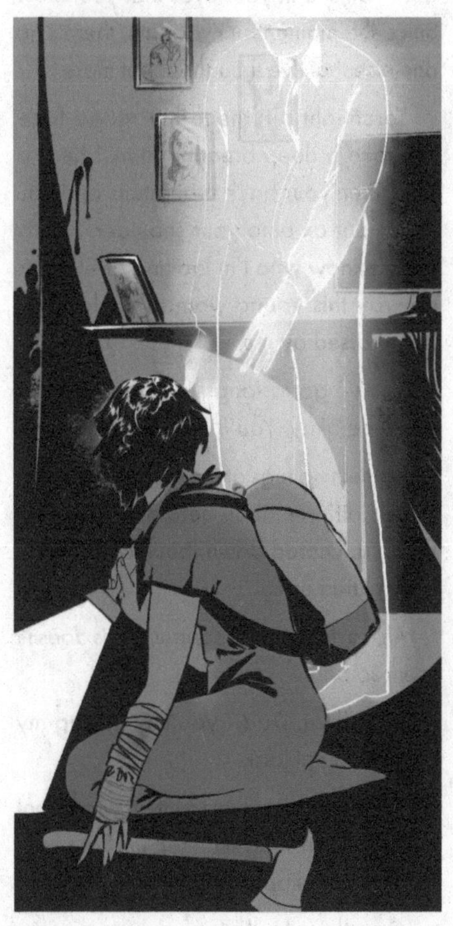

My smile wavers and falls. Reflexively, I want to argue, but it would be empty words. I've known for longer than death that you're right. Before, I didn't care. I thought I was providing. Now, with all the time in the world to think, I realise I was hiding behind that excuse.

"But I forgive you," you say, "because, in your own way, I know that..." Your torch trails along the walls, highlighting the photos of yourself. You don't finish the sentence, but I can see in your eyes that you know. Since the moment of my death, there's no one else that I've thought about more.

Torchlight returns to my rotted face. You take a deep breath. I think I hear a sniff. Then your back straightens and you hoist your ax onto your shoulder. Briefly, I don't know who I'm looking at—there's no way this young woman could have been raised by me.

You've got a long life ahead of you. You'll be okay. You'll do great.

Something tugs at me, gently but firmly. It feels different than before, not like I'm being anchored down, but more that I'm being lifted up.

Ah, so this is how it happens. This doesn't seem so bad.

"Goodbye, Dad," you say, giving my corpse a final look.

The tugging has turned into a wind, cool and sweet, growing stronger. The flat's floor has already slipped away from my feet.

"Goodbye, Holly."

A. KATHERINE BLACK

RECESSES OF URIEL

The silker sat alone in the middle of bridge twelve, a suspension she and Seventy-Six had spun years ago, a bridge that only moments ago had supported a heavy flow of handlers, headed to Uriel operations to receive their assignments for this cycle. A finger twirled one end of her braided silk belt, a souvenir from a recent bridge job.

Her two legs dangled over each side of the bridge, toes dancing against the depths. Wires strung above the bridge emitted a thin UV light that spilled over the silker before vanishing into the darkness beneath her feet. She watched the openings of the caves and tunnels dug into the wall of Uriel cavern, as genmods emerged from their pens, without her. Without Seventy-Six.

She'd rushed to the assignment room at the start of this cycle, pushing through the crowd, her meager human limbs twitching. Hoping she and Seventy-Six would be assigned to dark zone exploration again. She'd thought about taking another snack break during their exploration. Seventy-Six deserved it. No one had to know.

Beyond the entrance ledge of packed earth, inside the main cave, the boss had stood on her stool as always, thinly illuminated by grublights, tablet in hand.

Her voice echoed against the slick stone walls. Orders were issued. Cleaners wordlessly noted their assignments and peeled away toward the fish pens. Blockers went next, filing out to merge with their mites and begin their tasks. Carriers left for the beet pens, flyers for their bats.

Silk assignments always came last. The other silkers received their duties, one by one, and slipped away to merge with their racs, until she stood alone. The boss left the stool, came to meet her on the other side of the room.

"Bad slip," she'd said, eyes on the tablet. "First diagnostic on Seventy-Six was inconclusive. Keeper's re-checking systems. If equipment passes, means the rac's gone bad. Come back next cycle. Same rac or new rac, work'll be work."

That was it.

The boss walked off toward control, leaving the silker without her rac. Without Seventy-Six, the same rac she'd been handling for year upon year upon year. The assignment room was large enough for a rac to make a breezy jump on its eight legs from one end to the other, but it had felt small just then, holding only one human.

The silker had never left operations on only two legs, at the start of a work cycle. Seventy-Six remained in its pen, while she sat alone on a bridge of their making. With dull, insufficient eyes, she watched the other genmods as they poured out of their pens.

Every one of the creatures was larger than two humans, at least. Beets were as big as four. Red lights spread across the shadowed expanse, blinking on the necks of every genmod, signaling an active implant. The lone silker's neck ached for the weight of a helmet like those the handlers wore back in operations, as their genmods carried their minds out across the cavern for work—work feeble humans could never achieve on their own.

Fish, scaled legs and sucker limbs, slid across the cavern wall toward population center, to feed on unwanted moss and fungi in the habitats while humans worked elsewhere. Mites, their pincers snapping echoes across the vastness, split into two groups, some to fill cracks in the older habitat huts with regurgitated earth, others to shape bricks and stack them to dry near the lava tubes. Beets, their armored bodies colored in various shades of earth, trudged downward toward the lava tubes, to gather dried brick eady for delivery to the next construction zone. Bats dove and darted around stalactites just below the cavern ceiling, their black bodies only shadows against the faint sparkle of embedded crystals. Some glided in the direction of population center, others to the farthest reaches of the cavern, ready to receive and deliver messages of the cycle.

The racs were last to emerge. Always last, just in case an implant went bad and one of them decided to make a morsel of another genmod.

They spread out across the cavern walls and ceiling, abdomens and spinnerets bobbing as they disappeared in the near-black that blanketed everything outside population zone. Watching from her pathetic human body, she could almost feel the power of eight rac legs, the slight breeze of passing mods sending ripples across her rac's hairs, the deep black of the cavern transformed through rac eyes into rich greens and purples. Without her rac, the silker squinted from the bridge with blind humanity into the void, the beautiful colors of the dark taken from her.

⌛

Just last cycle she'd been with Seventy-Six, as usual. Moving beyond the weak grublights at population edge, they'd ventured into a far corner of the cavern in search of new anchor points. Their feet gripped damp walls as they searched the colorful darkness for smooth solid spots that might hold suspension silks for upcoming expansions.

The air tasted of wet and sulfur. They tapped the walls, feeling for vibrations, until they hit a hollow sound, indicating a cave or tunnel, drawing them in to investigate. The silker pushed her rac quickly toward the discovery, and they turned in.

A human might have stood upright in the tunnel. The silker could have, if she'd been there, instead of lying in a chair back in the merge-room, next to Seventy-Six's empty pen. But it was just the right size for the rac, who moved forward in spiral fashion, avoiding juts, unnecessarily breaking a few stalactites and stalagmites along the way.

For many rac lengths, the wall was cool to the touch. The heat came suddenly. Through rac eyes, the silker could see the wall glowing in a way that meant lava. And a bonus from the boss.

Relinquishing control slightly to Seventy-Six, the silker moved her fingers in her merge chair and tapped the com. She told the boss about the lava tube, not asking at the size of her bonus—that depended on econ factors the silker didn't care to understand. Any bump was good. Could garner a bigger hut, or at the smallest an extra bar visit or two.

Returning her mind to the rac after a near compliment from the boss, the silker found Seventy-Six tearing down the tunnel, away from the direction of Uriel Cavern, in pursuit of a tantalizing pattering of a thousand feet. Some sort of pede. Feeling as generous as the boss, the silker slipped back from Seventy-Six and let it dive into the hunt. She'd never been there for a meal. Forbidden, maybe, but she'd been a handler longer than not.

The kill was quick. A pede the size of the rac's leg was no match. Rac fangs pierced the creature's outer layer, as Seventy-Six began its meal. Subtle colors refracted through the pede's translucent body as it wriggled its final fight, all thousand legs kicking.

Pleasure hit the silker like a torrent as her rac sucked in luscious protein, wet and rich. Satisfaction erupted like nothing else. She tingled from head to toe. The rac leaned closer into its kill, enveloping it with front legs, and the silker felt herself slip back into the human body. Images flickered. Urges. Wanting. Needing. Running.

A voice broke into the com next to the silker's human head.

"Connection with Seventy-Six lost. What's going on out there?"

The silker just got a pay bump a few breaths ago. Bad slip to ruin the celebration with details.

"Dunno. Nothing. Lost contact." Two arms and two legs limp against the merge chair.

"Drones bound for last signal locale. Hold for re-connect."

She lay in her chair, merge helmet snapped onto her implant, waiting for input. UV light fell from a seam in the ceiling, chasing her eyes to a corner of the room before she succumbed and closed them, recalling the rush of that kill.

Less than a quarter cycle later, she guided Seventy-Six back to its pen. After drones found the new tunnel and reconnected the silker with her rac, she'd been ordered to bring it back for diagnostics. They could have crawled back along the wall, but, still feeling the rush of the kill, the silker and her rac made several leaps through the wide open space of the cavern, savoring the expanse below their eight legs, before nearing population center and operations.

Back in the pen, the silker looked through rac eyes at her human body on the other side of the window, reclined in the merge chair, revoltingly soft. She slipped out of the rac and into that body, unsnapped her helmet and sat, looking at the rac look back at her.

"Silker, report to med room for implant impedance check," said the com.

She headed for the door, opened it, and closed it, still in the room. The UV light turned off, tricked, leaving only the weak glow of a small grublight hanging on the wall. The rac shifted to face the silker by the door. Dim light reflected off every one of its eyes.

A hatch opened on the other end of the pen, and in dropped a smaller spider. Not a complex genmod like the racs, only a simple mod, for larger size, about half that of a human. Livestock. Seventy-six turned immediately.

The chase was short, up and around the side of the pen, ending with a cracking sound the silker could hear through glass. She watched the rac devour yet another meal, breathing in the moist earth on her side of the window, remembering the taste of that earlier kill. She swallowed.

"Silker, you're wanted in med room."

■

A cycle later, the silker was alone, without her rac. Sitting on a bridge they built together, her insides awash with the thrill of the hunt, and tense with understanding of Seventy-Six's fate. A fate that loomed not because of the rac's actions, but because of the silker's choice, because the silker let Seventy-Six roam as a free rac, if for only a few breaths. The silker's insides calmed as she stood and headed toward population edge, to wait for the next cycle, when the keeper would be off-duty.

■

The keeper was always in the same cheap bar where most keepers and handlers spent their pay. Walking across suspension bridge one-oh-eight, the silker ran her fingers along the interwoven threads of the bridge's handle, feeling the strength of rac silk, fingers dancing over every intricate knot tied by Seventy-Six, under the silker's direction.

She paused in a dark section of the bridge, just outside the flood of the bar's UV lights. Closing her eyes and gripping the bridge's threads, she felt the chaotic vibrations pouring out from the bar. People moving around each other, against each other, away from each other. She wanted to settle into that moment, standing on silk, nestled in darkness. But she had to move.

UV lights hung in disarray inside the bar, casting odd shadows. Moss grew thick on the walls and the edges of tables. Keeping this place clean was not a priority. The keeper was in a back corner, sitting in front of two overturned mugs, a third in hand.

The silker went to the bar, entered her name and order on the console and waited for someone to slap her drinks on the counter. She drained the first mug, savoring the burn of bitter moss spirit creeping down her gullet, before grabbing the second and weaving through the crowd toward the keeper.

"Seat open?"

The keeper looked up from his drink and paused, lingering on the silker's face before nodding toward a stool across the table. This wasn't the first time they'd sat together.

The silker took the seat next to him instead. They sipped their drinks in silence, letting the noise from the operations crowd fill the space between them. Their mugs were half drained when the keeper spoke.

"Seems Seventy-Six'll be scrapped." He took a sip, not looking at the silker who'd merged with Seventy-Six for over a decade. "Rough slot."

The silker's movements slowed. Her back curled. Her head throbbed with the pulse of bodies moving around the bar. Any of them would be easily snapped, easily drained by Seventy-Six. Her molten heart erupted, spreading, shifting hot beneath her skin.

The keeper tilted his head to drain the last of the moss spirit from his mug. His neck shone bare, soft. Setting down his overturned mug next to the others, he pushed back his stool. The silker reached out. Brushed the skin on the back of the keeper's arm. Muscle shuddered beneath the silker's human fingers. Her hand traveled, lingering on the center of the keeper's back before crawling up to the neck, and curving around to run along the collar bone. Blood pulsed under the silker's touch.

The keeper knew the silker's touch, or thought he did.

"My hut isn't far," he said.

She slid her own mug, spirit still inside, up against the others. "I know a better place."

They crossed the bridge in silence, hands reaching out, exploring curves beneath clothing, until they arrived at the entrance of an unfinished cave, slotted for development in the months ahead.

They faced each other under the glow of the last grublight, inhaling scents of fungus and earth, sweat and spirit. The silker loosened her belt under the keeper's gaze, then grabbed his arm to draw him deeper into darkness. When only the faintest outline of the keeper was visible, the silker advanced, pushing him against the damp wall of unpacked earth.

She kissed his neck, raked her teeth against vulnerable skin, as she untied the front of his shirt. The keeper's ragged breath rippled across the soft hairs on her check. She flipped him, pressing his chest against raw earth. Slipping his shirt over his shoulders, her mouth worked down his spine as she gathered his arms, hands trapped in his sleeves. The keeper moaned as her mouth lingered at the small of his back, as her fingers tied the spider silk belt around his wrists.

Deft as any silker in the cavern, even without a rac's limbs at her disposal, she swiftly wrapped it next around his ankles.

She stood, and with one strong tug, the keeper's feet lifted from the ground to join with his wrists. He fell with a grunt.

⧗

It was a slow move across the construction section of the cavern, now shut down for sleepcycle and only sparsely lit with grubs. The silker cursed her weak, soft body as she slowly dragged the keeper across loose earth, his weight resisting forward motion.

He said nothing, stifled his grunts. A good keeper knew when the hunt was over.

Sticking to the shadows as much as possible, save for a few tense moments crossing suspension bridges eight and sixty-two, the silker arrived at the back entrance, where keepers accessed the genmod pens.

She loosened the binding on the keeper's wrists and heaved him up and sideways. He groaned as she raised one of his hands in what must have been a painful angle, high enough to reach the scanner. A red warning light appeared. No access.

She pulled the keeper's arms higher behind his back, bringing the other hand toward the scanner. He resisted, leaned his head away from the door, until an odd pop echoed against the empty air, and he yelled. His resistance gave way. His shoulder jutted out strangely under his skin. She pressed the other hand against the scanner. A click sounded.

She pushed the door open and dragged the keeper through.

Cursing her human muscles, the silker bent and grabbed the keeper's good arm to drag him further in. Faint lighting in the tunnels forced her to squint at labels as she passed pen after pen, interspersed with control modules. Genmods rippled and twitched behind doors. Swooping flutters from the bat pens overhead, abrasive rubbing from the mite pens underfoot, heavy sounds of scaled bodies sliding against packed dirt in the fish pens on either side, until, finally, they reached the rac section.

The keeper moaned, shifted against the silker's pull.

She walked faster, thighs burning. She needed her rac. She dropped the keeper and grabbed a grubbag from the wall. Holding the dim light up to door after door, she found Seventy-Six. A slash chalked across its number, with writing underneath. *Scrap.*

She found the nearest console and began tapping. *Training procedures... short-range mergecoms...* And there it was. A green light blinked against a map of the docking bay and pens. Just a few doors away, shelves that held training equipment.

Movement sounded behind Seventy-Six's door. She almost spoke to her rac. Almost there, she would have said. But she'd never spoken to Seventy-Six out loud. Something wrong about starting that now.

Using the grubbag, she reached the shelves within minutes and tore through sacks until she found what she recognized from her old training days. Dumping the grubs from the bag, she filled it with the equipment they'd need.

Making her way back to her rac, she saw the keeper was gone. Drag marks on the dirt told he went deeper in, toward the docking bay. No time to bother.

The silker worked the console again, first with a quick impedance check on Seventy-Six's implant. Connection still good. Then a check on the receiver. Also good. Disable long-range reception. Done.

Activating one of the short-range transmitters she'd just found, the silker slipped it over her head. It slid onto her own implant connections and snapped in place. A deep buzz rang in her head, irritating. Her right eyelid to twitched. No connection.

She stepped to Seventy-Six's door, leaning her entire body against it. Her senses expanded. She saw the beautiful dark of the pen, full spectrum of blues and greens and grays. She felt her human heart beating on the other side of the doorway. Her rac placed a leg against the door, and the thump came through, loud and full.

Senses slipped again, and she was back to her small, thin body, dulled, darkness closing in. She'd have to get closer to make the connection.

The silker stepped back, tying a bag of extra equipment to her belt. Her first-year instructor's yells came back to her, from all those years ago. "No one ever opens a door to an uncontrolled mod! You got that?" And the class always yelled back, "Sir, yes, sir!" And the silker opened the door.

A sweet, potent stench of blood and iron spilled out of the pen. Darkness remained. Several large round eyes of varying sizes reflected dim grublight from the middle of the pen. They stood, the two, unmoving. She wondered if it remembered her from the other side of the window. She remembered the joy it felt, they felt, at capturing the pede in the dark zone.

She took a step forward. The rac stepped forward as well. It would be a tight fit through the door meant for humans, but she knew Seventy-Six could do it. Slowly moving a hand to her helmet, she tapped the search button again.

She stumbled as her senses fell in and out. The world flipped, from clear and crisp to dull and soft, as her mind jumped between her human self and her rac. On unsteady legs, she stepped forward until she was in the doorway. Either Seventy-Six was going to eat her and escape, or it was going to merge. And escape.

Her senses fell back into the rac. For a split second, she saw her human body, and something rising behind it. Two hands. A rock.

She fell back into that body, her movements stunted, disoriented from the back and forth.

Before she could react, Seventy-Six jumped toward her. One of its front legs grabbed and gripped her torso, burning where the millions of tiny hairs sunk through her clothing and into her skin. Still in forward motion, it threw her to the side and landed on top of the keeper. His scream pierced the empty halls and quickly drowned to a gurgle.

A loud crunch, and the keeper became another meal for rac number seventy-six.

The silker lay on the floor of the pen, listening to the crack and slurp for a few seconds before she stood, carefully, and approached the back of the rac. Their equipment made connection. She flew into its senses, seeing the broken body in front of their pincers, seeing the human standing at the rac's side, torn clothing, scraped face, vacant eyes.

The silker pulled herself back slightly into the human mind, just enough to propel her weak, soft legs onto the wide rounded body of the rac, sitting in the nook between the thorax and the abdomen. Rough hairs pierced her skin. She lay just below the back eyes and reached her arms out, bracing herself against Seventy-Six's body. Sinking back into the rac's senses, they finished their meal, drinking the sweet rich syrup of the former keeper.

Pulling silk from their spinneret and fluffing it against their back legs, they secured the human body against the rac. Stepping over the empty corpse of the keeper, they crawled through the tunnel, past the other pens, until they emerged into the cavern. They headed away from the harsh lights of the human city, toward the dark zone.

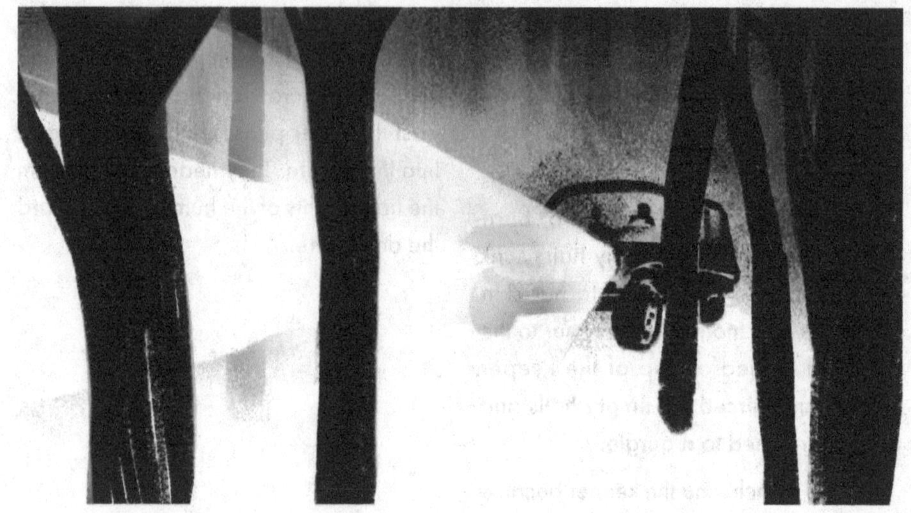

HAILEY PIPER

PLEASANT GUESTS WITH BETTER GAMES

Kneeling at the picture window this Christmas Eve reminded Catherine of standing in line for the carnival rollercoaster last summer, eager to reach the line's front, dreading the ride. Tonight, she wanted Diedre to arrive, and yet Catherine's nerves twisted, tight as pulled hair.

The weeks between Diedre's leaving for college and her miserable Thanksgiving visit had felt eternal, the silent month since even longer. This visit would be better. Christmas beat Thanksgiving every time.

When headlights glared through the glass, that pulled-hair tension snapped at its root. Catherine couldn't help squealing, "She's here!"

Mom shouted from the kitchen about calming down, forgetting Catherine was eight. No kid slept on Christmas Eve, let alone calmed down. Dad's chair groaned at his rising as if it already missed him, and he turned off the TV where the angry channel growled at all hours.

The headlights cast shadows from thick snowflakes before winking out. Despite a veil of white wind, Catherine eyed Diedre's small forest-green junker, its snow-speckled windshield, and the occupied front seats. She counted the figures before Mom opened her mouth.

"There's someone else," Mom whispered. A moment later: "A girl."

"But you told her not to bring that Kya again," Dad said, sounding exhausted. "Rex was bad enough at Thanksgiving."

Catherine remembered that. She also remembered Dad joining along in Uncle Rex's ribbing of Diedre's guest. That was Rex's word—ribbing—which Mom said meant poking fun.

Diedre and Kya weren't having fun. Catherine couldn't understand everything said, but she noticed when words that made Dad and Rex laugh set Kya's eyes downcast and Diedre's shoulders shaking. Neither said a word, not even goodbye when they changed plans from staying the weekend to driving away that night.

Catherine should have spoken up, said something cute or funny to heal the holiday. She would keep an eye on Uncle Rex, Dad, everyone this time. Best behavior tonight. Christmas Eve law demanded it.

"It's Christmas," she said without turning around.

Dad's reflection straightened its back, potato chip crumbs falling from its flannel button-down. Mom's reflection smoothed out its Christmas sweater, lined with smiling reindeer.

The front door creaked open, winter's wind shouting *I'm home!* before Diedre had the chance.

Her round face flushed red with cold, and white flakes rained from her jeans and black hoodie. She began to stamp snow off her boots.

Catherine weaved past her parents to hug Diedre first, and then Dad swooped in. Mom pouted over getting the last hug.

"The last one deserves it most," Diedre said, her face cloaked in Mom's auburn hair. Her smile shone through, and had the night frozen then, Catherine could have called this a perfect Christmas Eve.

Instead, she asked "Is Kya coming?"

The hug melted as Diedre slid back to the door. "No, Cat. Kya's spending Christmas with her cousin. She got Thanksgiving's message loud and clear."

The front door pressed inward behind her, and another woman her age slid through. She dressed in a dark sweater and skirt with thick leggings. She had the widest eyes, wet and golden as honey. No backpack or purse swung from her shoulder.

"Anna's my plus-one," Diedre said. "Just a dorm friend."

Those last few words kept the smiles on Mom's and Dad's faces.

Anna mimicked them with scrunched cheeks. "Happy holidays!" she shouted, waving an enthusiastic hand.

Stairway steps cried, and a gruff throat cleared. Catherine didn't look from the living room foyer to the stairs; she *felt*

Uncle Rex descend, a man tall and bald as a mountain. She fell under his shadow as he approached the new houseguest.

A grimace crossed his freshly shaved face. "Merry Christmas," he said, knuckles rubbing the hips of his jeans. "You mean."

The air chilled, Anna's smile frozen stiff. "Same thing, right?"

"No, young lady. It isn't."

Dad opened his mouth to say something, but Rex's chest puffed out, and Dad shrank back. In some ways, younger siblings remained small forever.

"Back in the day," Rex said, with a pause for reverence. "Back then, we had a little something called Christmas spirit. Wasn't some frivolous holiday to throw with the others. Not that you'd remember."

Catherine held still, skin frozen as if Diedre and Anna had let in all of winter before they shut the front door.

Anna's toothy grin shattered the ice. "Well, Merry Christmas then."

Rex plodded close, slippers crushing snow, and then a laugh quaked up his chest. "I like this girl," he said, and his tree trunk arms wrapped her in a hug. "I'm just ribbing you."

Everyone chuckled, even Catherine, but her gut said that he wouldn't have been ribbing if Anna hadn't said that magic word. Christmas held that kind of power.

While Mom gave Anna the downstairs tour, Dad returned to the living room, and Uncle Rex followed. Catherine rarely heard the word "Christmas" from the TV speakers. Sometimes the angry channel gave "immigrant" this and "trans" that. Though she didn't know their meanings, her dad and uncle soaked rage into their spongy heads, processed it into trembling fear, and then radiated anger back, a cycle between their skin and the screen. Catherine preferred books over Christmas specials, freeing the TV for Dad's and Rex's frequent absorption.

"Nothing against the LG-whatevers," Rex said, his recliner creaking on the far side of the couch from Dad's.

"Nope," Dad said.

"Just no need for your kid to shove it down our throats during family time. It's Christmas, for God's sake."

There, the magic word, but Rex couldn't cheer himself up. He needed someone else to say it. Catherine started toward the sofa to wish him a merry one when Diedre stormed past, shoulders hunched. She ducked into Anna's dark hair and whispered, "Don't wait," and then she slipped into the downstairs bathroom and shut the door.

Catherine hadn't realized she needed to go until then. That had to be a sister thing, as if Diedre's return helped Catherine know herself better. She scurried upstairs and into the bathroom there.

Voices didn't follow until she finished washing her hands.

"This is the guest bedroom?" That was Anna, her tone honey-sweet. Heavy footsteps walked with her.

"Mine," Uncle Rex said, a laugh in his voice. "I mean, you're welcome to share, but think you'll take Diedre's old room. She'll bunk with Cat."

"Welcome to share." Anna almost sang the words.

Catherine flicked off the bathroom light, turned the doorknob, and opened the door a crack. The upstairs hall loomed dark from here, the faint light from downstairs broken by Anna's slender silhouette and Rex's mountainous shadow.

Anna's darkness turned to Rex, chin jutting up at him. "You seem quite giving. You remember old days and honor them." Her fist reached for his neck.

Rex stiffened. "I mean, 'tis the season, but I was just ribbing about sharing. You're what, how old?"

"Very old," Anna said. Her silhouette shifted, and her fist uncurled into a long-nailed hand. She wrenched it back from Rex with a wet slash.

Catherine started to shout, but nervous icicles pierced her tongue. No sound rushed out, only breath.

Rex groaned, stumbled back, and then pitched forward into Anna's arms. Slender as branches, she somehow cradled the mountain. "Poor little Rex," she said. "Always harder on the aged, so sleep the sleep of kings."

The non-scream had taken all of Catherine's breath. She couldn't help inhaling, sudden and quick, and her gasp sent whistling wind through her throat.

Anna glared up from Rex's shadow, and despite the upstairs darkness, her eyes glowed golden as headlights.

At Catherine.

She slammed the bathroom door and twisted its lock. The breath she'd taken turned to ice in her chest. No, she hadn't seen a claw scratch Rex's throat. No, she hadn't seen Anna's eyes glow. Not tonight.

"It's Christmas," Catherine whispered, and she listened for the world to calm down. "Nothing's bad at Christmas."

A banging fist sent the door quivering. "Cat?" Anna called.

Catherine scrambled backward through the dark bathroom until her spine struck and chilled against the window wall. Its glass breathed cold between the towel rack and shower curtain. She tried to hold hers, as if that would stop her heart from racing.

It only pounded harder, same as Anna's fist on the door. "Kitty-Cat, your uncle and I—it's a Christmas game," Anna said. A faint line of light crossed beneath the bathroom door, broken by the shadows of two slender legs.

Catherine's breath wouldn't hold; her lungs were like cats, in and out, never satisfied. Wind rushed through her teeth, and frost ate across her skull as if she'd bitten into an ice cream scoop.

Anna patted the door, gently now. "Don't you know they used to play games at Christmas back in the day?"

Those last four words.

They meant something to Catherine's family, at least to Rex, and maybe if she understood them, Christmas Eve might still be okay. Not perfect, but okay.

The icicles released Catherine's tongue. "When Uncle Rex was little?" she asked.

"No, Kitty-Cat, when *I* was little," Anna said. Her voice became wispy, and she began to pace the bathroom door's line of light. "Truly back in the day, when Christmas was young and we adored its games, or perhaps Christmas happened to come when we played in the winter and hunted men for sport. There was tag, snowball fights—you know those, but have you heard of the switch game?"

Catherine shook her head and then realized Anna couldn't see.

But Anna answered as if she could. "In those days, villages sometimes banished neighbors for sin, or perceived sin, or too little sin. For a myriad of reasons, banishers sent the banished into our woods to die. That was their custom."

Nails scraped down the door, likely slick with Uncle Rex's blood.

When Anna's pacing legs stepped left, a third limb blotted the faint line of light,

and a fourth, and then her shadow blackened Catherine's tiny bathroom world.

"But they likewise kept the custom of guest right," Anna said. "Anyone who came to their home seeking shelter would know welcoming and kindness. When we played the switch game, we played on this custom. In exchange for our woods taking the banished, one of us switched, took their place in the village, and demanded guest right. We were pleasant guests, the kind you'd like, Kitty-Cat. We would bear gifts, like I have tonight."

Light returned beneath the door as shadows merged into two legs and stepped away.

"A gift for Rex," Anna sang, voice fading. "A gift for Mommy and Daddy. A gift for you."

Catherine's back froze to the wall. She listened to the movement of a heavy, soft burden, and then the stairs creaked gently. Anna descended, but not Uncle Rex.

Catherine waited until certain she was alone, and then she unlocked and opened the bathroom door. The dark hall hung empty.

No Anna.

No Rex. His guest bedroom door stood shut. Catherine pressed an ear to the wood, but nothing breathed inside that she could hear. Her fingers danced toward the knob. If Uncle Rex lay inside, she could open the door and see what kind of gift Anna had given him.

     PLEASANT GUESTS WITH BETTER GAMES

Catherine's fingers dropped. She didn't want to see for herself. She wanted Mom.

She hugged the wall opposite the stairway banister and shuffled step by cautious step, in case Anna might be listening below. No one waited at the bottom. The bathroom door remained shut. Was Diedre still inside, or had she switched with someone else?

In the living room, Dad still watched the angry channel alone. He didn't seem to notice or care that Rex was gone. No Anna here. Next, the dining room, the kitchen—Anna had vanished. She had to be the one in the downstairs bathroom, maybe cleaning Rex's blood off her fingers.

Diedre stood by the oven, a ladle in one hand, Mom draped over her shoulder and whispering into her curly hair. A steel pot burbled from the stovetop, drowning Mom's every word. They had no idea what had happened to Rex.

"Merry Christmas," Catherine whispered to herself, and then she crept toward the oven.

Anna swept past, chilly as winter's wind, and her nail prodded between Catherine's shoulders. Her fingers looked clean.

"Mrs. Campbell, I spilled something upstairs," she said. "Can you show me which towels to use? I don't want to ruin the good linens." She spun away, eyes spitting honey at Catherine before she bounded back upstairs.

Mom patted Diedre's shoulder and muttered, "Mrs. Campbell." She half-laughed as she turned to the living room on her way out of the kitchen. "Makes me sound like your mother!" Dad's mumbled reply died between walls.

Mom was about to climb the stairs when Catherine caught the hem of her sweater in small fingers. A scowling *What?* painted Mom's face.

Catherine shook her head, but icicles had driven through her tongue again and she couldn't shake the words loose. Rex. Claws. The switch game. Their family had banished Kya, and now Anna had taken her place. Couldn't Mom read Catherine's fear? Shouldn't mothers have that power to instinctively know when something was wrong?

Mom bent down, kissed the top of Catherine's head, and hurried up the stairs. "One moment, Anna."

And then she was gone.

No Rex, no Mom.

Catherine listened for a scratch, a groan, anything. If Mom gave sounds of distress, they stayed upstairs, perhaps looking out the window for when Santa would deliver kinder gifts than Anna's.

Or would he, too, be switched, some horned, hairy monster taking his place?

Catherine turned from the stairs and spotted Dad staring at her from the living room. Angry people called his attention back to the TV after a moment, every word spitting fear inside him. But that was just TV. He should have been afraid of this stranger that Diedre had let into the house.

Catherine ambled into the kitchen and tugged Diedre's hoodie. "Where's Kya?"

"At her cousin's." Diedre ran the heel of her palm down one tearstained cheek. "I told you, remember?"

"Why didn't you bring her?" Catherine asked. Icicles lifted from her tongue, and she made herself swallow them to speak plainly. "I don't like the switch game. Anna isn't nice."

Diedre's face seemed to hang off her skull. "No, she isn't."

Catherine chilled again. Diedre knew all about Anna.

"Then why?" Catherine asked.

Diedre knelt, eyes meeting Catherine's. Their whites ran red.

"Dad, Mom, Uncle Rex—for them, every Christmas comes in a thin glass box. Hold it too tight, you'll crack the glass. Hold it too loose, it'll tumble and shatter. Hold it secure, and your fingers will smudge the surface, so you'll constantly and carefully rotate the box while wiping the sides. Smudge, wipe, over and over. For them, no matter what you do with the Christmas box, you're doing it wrong. Do you understand?"

New icicles pierced Catherine's tongue. She shook her head.

"If I can't hold the box right, no matter what, I'd rather chuck it at the wall and smash it into a thousand pieces." Diedre squeezed Catherine's shoulder, eyes wet with tears, and then turned to the kitchen doorway.

Anna had returned. Her fingers ran red; she hadn't bothered to wash them this time.

"Mom?" Diedre asked.

"You know it," Anna said. Headlight eyes flashed to Catherine. "And the kitten?"

"Not here. I want him to see." Diedre offered her hand to Catherine, hoodie sleeve dangling, and for a moment she looked as hopeful as she had on Thanksgiving when she first brought Kya to the house. That night had turned brittle and broken apart later, but briefly, Diedre had seemed oblivious to unhappy futures.

Same as Catherine earlier tonight. Neither of them had stayed that way. These holidays had switched hope for dread, and no wishing anyone a merry Christmas could switch things back. She grasped Diedre's hand, and they followed Anna into the living room. Dad looked oblivious, too, as if the angry channel had changed its broadcast from fear-inducing to hypnotic.

Anna broke the hypnosis when she shut the TV off.

Dad looked around, bewildered. "Did Liz call dinner and I didn't hear?"

"Mom didn't say a word, Dad," Diedre said, joining Anna between the darkened television and Dad's recliner. "But I have a few."

Dad nestled back, his jaw set. He didn't know what to expect, did he? Catherine didn't either, she realized. Her gaze swept from father to sister to the stranger who didn't fit.

"I thought things would be different when I brought Kya home," Diedre said, dropping Catherine's hand. "I thought none of you would say and think the things you're told to say and think if you knew the truth about me. Pretty pathetic, huh? No matter how awful things get, I keep trying to catch a family joy that I barely remember ever feeling." Her head cocked in Catherine's direction. "Maybe since I was her age."

A curse slid through Catherine's heart. All of eight years old, this Christmas Eve was the last she would remember feeling family joy. Even that had crumbled from the start, everything going wrong since Diedre's snowy homecoming.

Or had everything always been wrong, with Catherine too young to notice?

Dad's eyes flickered, weathered with strain. "You done?" he asked, and then chinned at Anna. "So, what? You're with her now?"

"No, I'm still with Kya," Diedre said softly. "But I didn't bring her here again. Anna had a better idea."

Anna's smirk curled. "Gifts." She licked her front teeth.

Dad seemed to notice her red hands now, and he shot up from his groaning seat.

"What did you do?" He pressed past the furniture toward the stairs. "Liz? Rex?"

The words snaked through Catherine's lips. "They're dead."

Diedre shushed, and Anna slinked close to Catherine.

"They aren't dead," Anna said. "Just sleeping. Why don't we wake them?"

Her body curled at the middle, an organic musical instrument, and a shrill note whistled between her lips, wind through skeletal branches.

The steps cried beneath heavy footsteps, much like when Uncle Rex would descend. Catherine turned, the chill leaving her skin. Maybe dread could switch back with hope after all. Games ended, even the switch game.

Hope died in her chest as legs lurched into view. She couldn't count them, their numbers lost in a forest of scraggly hair that writhed and twisted, a living thing having overtaken two bodies and reshaped their flesh and bone into lupine forms. They walked side by side, yellow claws tearing from the end of every limb. No snout or jaw jutted from either head, only a damp, gaping hole ringed with pointy teeth.

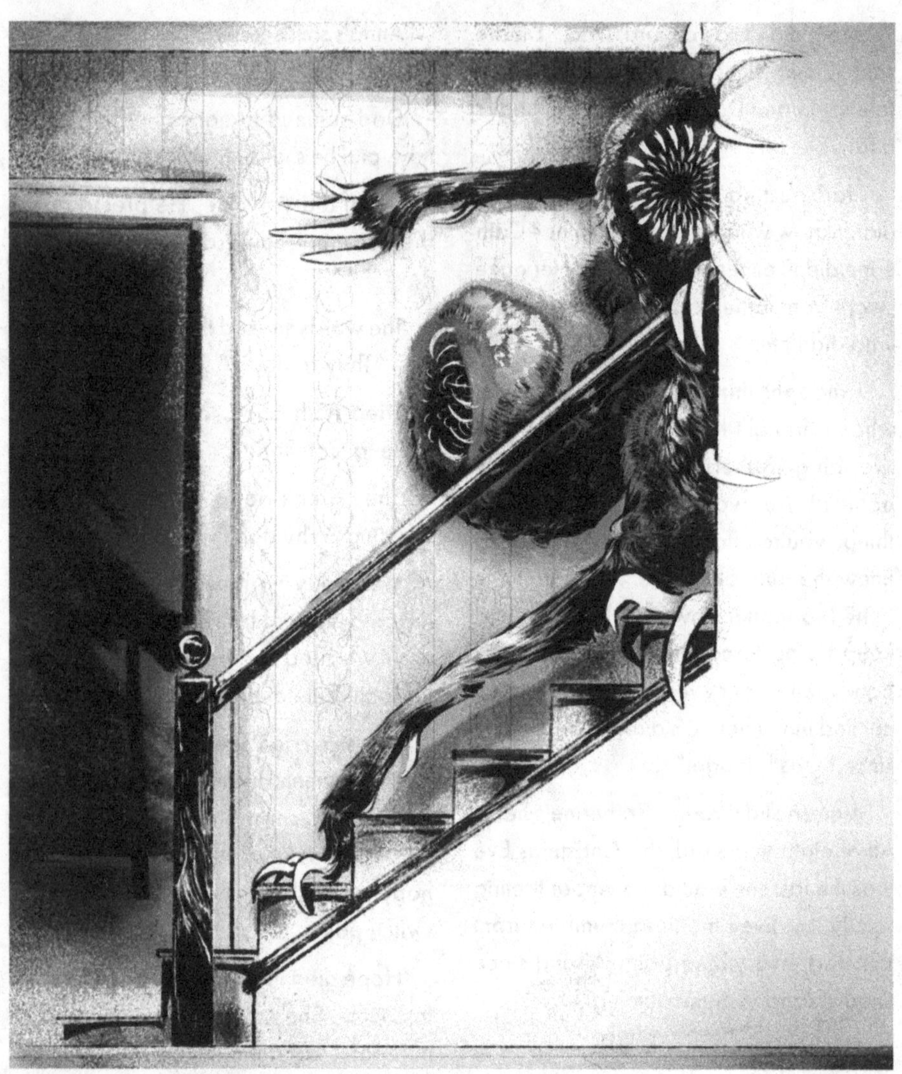

Dad fell back, knocking his faithful recliner aside, and scrambled backward on all fours until he slammed against the entertainment unit. Words sputtered on his lips, a fire that couldn't catch in winter's cold.

Catherine's blood ran icy, eyes fixed first on the dark pits in those strange heads, and then on the torn bits of fabric tangled in their hair. Bits of denim. Scraps of brown wool that had once shaped reindeer. She understood the switch game better now. No one had to explain to her who these creatures used to be.

Red fingers grasped Catherine's shoulder, and she looked up, caught in Anna's smirking shadow.

PLEASANT GUESTS WITH BETTER GAMES

"Be nice," Deidre said, a cry caught tight in her throat. Anna didn't look her way, honey eyes now melting over Catherine.

"Let's play a Christmas game, Kitty-Cat," she said. "This time, with Daddy."

Dad trembled on the floor, lips now spitting, desperate for words. With the angry channel silent, he seemed hollowed out, an emptiness as dark and damp as the toothy gaps in Mom's and Rex's faces.

"Bet you wish I'd brought Kya, huh?" Diedre asked. Tears ran freely down her cheeks, only interrupted where her smile echoed Anna's.

"I don't like the switch game," Catherine said, as if what she wanted still mattered this Christmas.

"The game's almost over," Anna said.

She mimicked the gentle squeeze that Diedre had given Catherine's shoulder, and then a sharp nail traced Catherine's neck. Anna had scratched the same on Mom and Uncle Rex. Catherine's icy blood melted in a hot rush. Had she been older, maybe the force of it would have knocked her out.

But she was eight, and no kid slept on Christmas Eve.

"This game's different," Anna went on. "The banished runs, same as with the switch game, but now the banishers chase him."

She faced Dad as the hairy figures clambered over recliner and sofa, stinking like wet dog, their mouths begging to swallow the world. Dad's eyes jittered every which way. He didn't know where to look. Where was safe anymore?

He at last seemed more afraid than the TV words could make him.

Anna cupped a hand beneath his chin and forced his gaze to her. "Back in the day, when I was little, your kind kept the custom of guest right. And in fairness, your family has been kind to me." Her fingers splayed, careful not to scratch Dad's skin. "Me," she repeated, harsher.

"But Kya," Diedre said, gaze piercing Dad as if her eyes were icicles and he were a tongue. "Uncle Rex was bad, always has been, but you should've stuck up for me. Doesn't matter who's older, you should've had a will. Should've been a father."

"A host," Anna said. "When it comes to Kya, you broke the custom of guest right. You long for the old days, yes? Back in the day, breaking custom had consequences. And back in the day, we played games at Christmas."

Dad jerked his face out of Anna's grasp and began crawling backward again, first along the entertainment unit and then toward one wall. If he didn't look back, maybe he would find some secret exit.

He went still when his gaze fell on Catherine, and a low moan tore up his throat.

Scraggly hair bloomed down her arms. Bones split through her body, too numb with cold to feel pain. Her fingers stretched long and pointy. She glanced to Anna and Diedre to say that Dad used to read to her, that he was a nice dad and cared about them, even if he was weak and cowardly. She started to say "It's Christmas," as if that could still pacify the world.

Instead her jaw sank into her face, her tongue drooped, and the icicles that once silenced her now spread in a circle of teeth. Dad didn't look much like himself anymore. He looked like game, from back in the day when Anna was little and her kind hunted men for sport. Catherine could almost feel the trees and snow.

"Now then, let's play," Anna said, smirking once more. "Kitty-Cat, show Daddy your claws."

PAUL C.K. SPEARS

BUREAUCRACY OF WEIRD
"A MATTER OF NATIONAL SECURITY"

2021 was a turbulent year, for UFO news. Previously, we covered the story of Lue Elizondo, the leader of a secret UFO program within the Department of Defense. Originally sponsored by late senator Harry Reid[1], Elizondo's program (known as AATIP) seems to have lasted from around 2007 to 2014, before it expired due to lack of funding.

Around this point, Elizondo leaked the GOFAST, GIMBAL and FLIR videos[2] to the public. These videos are now available on YouTube, and the DOD has confirmed they are legitimate[3]. After the videos leaked, *The New York Times* ran an expose on the secret project[4], and the DOD was finally pressured into presenting a report on UFOs[5]—now rebranded as "UAPs," or "Unidentified Aerial Phenomenon," by the military.

This step took the United States into uncharted waters. The U.S. government, after 70 years, had finally admitted the presence of strange, unidentified objects in American airspace.

But as always with UAPs, a certain level of mystery remained.

In the controversy after the *New York Times* story, two major questions rose to the surface. One: What were these things, and where had they come from? And two: What the hell was the DOD going to do about their presence in American airspace?

It didn't take long for that second question to reach the mainstream.

In 2021, an oddball group of Senators managed to squeeze UAP-related amendments into the 2022 National Defense Spending Act (NDAA)[6], and demanded DOD accountability around UAP's. This thrust them into confrontation with military leadership, and a secret war erupted between elected officials and the Pentagon.

This battle raged quietly, behind the scenes, but the details are all a matter of public record. Here's how it all went down...

---

1   The Hill, "Reinvigorating the UAP legacy of Sen. Harry Reid"

2   Wikipedia, "Pentagon UFO Videos"

3   The Guardian, "Pentagon Confirms Leaked Photos And Video Of UFOs Are Legitimate"

4   The New York Times, "Glowing Auras and 'Black Money': The Pentagon's Mysterious U.F.O. Program"

5   US Office of National Intelligence, "Preliminary Assessment: Unidentified Aerial Phenomena"

6   Ruben Gallego, "PASSED: Rep. Ruben Gallego NDAA Amendment on Unidentified Aerial Phenomena"

Change doesn't happen in a vacuum. The government showdown over UAPs was catalyzed by a June 2021 defense report[7], ordered by Congress. Elected officials had seen the leaked UAP videos, and they had questions. Lots of questions.

Congress was hoping for answers, some sort of logical explanation. Maybe these objects were all just secret military planes, or maybe they were some sort of foreign drones. Surely the DOD would pony up the data, now that they were under pressure.

Instead of answers, they got... Well, not much. When the report arrived, it did not contain the information Congress or the public had been looking for. The declassified version of the report[8] confirmed a number of UAP sightings by the military, and indeed, many of these could not be conventionally explained[9]. Some UAPs demonstrated accelerations and speeds beyond those of any known military craft, as well as a notable lack of exhaust, lack of external sensory equipment, or even a visible means of propulsion. In a word, some sightings were truly bizarre—almost impossible to explain with conventional, current military technology or natural phenomena.

But when it came to the nature of these sightings, and potential explanations, the military was less than helpful.

In the June report's own words: "The limited amount of high-quality reporting on unidentified aerial phenomena (UAP) hampers our ability to draw firm conclusions about the nature or intent of UAP... We currently lack sufficient information in our dataset to attribute incidents to specific explanations."

This kind of wishy-washy language was not a good look for the DOD. The same people Congress handed billions of dollars in defense money to every year, had just given them an intelligence report on UAPs concluding with "I dunno." This should be disturbing to any American taxpayer, especially after recent reports of UAPs buzzing Navy vessels off the coast of California[10]. As a former Defense Department official, Christopher Mellon, put it[11]: "the inability of [the DOD] to engage effectively on the [UFO] issue is why so little has changed or been accomplished since 2004."

Several Senators—including Kirsten Gillibrand and Marco Rubio—became more outspoken about the UAP issue as 2021 went on. In Rubio's own words[12], "There's stuff flying in our airspace, and

---

7   *Office of the Director of National Security, "Preliminary Assessment: Unidentified Aerial Phenomena"*

8   *US Office of National Intelligence, "Preliminary Assessment: Unidentified Aerial Phenomena"*

9   *The Hill, "Are UFOs From Outer Space? Key Questions The Uap Report Left Unanswered"*

10   *The Hill, "UFOs, the Channel Islands And The Navy's 'Drone Swarm' Mystery"*

11   *The Hill, "Ex-Officials Voice Deep Concerns Over New Pentagon Ufo Unit"*

12   *Politico, "'We've Got To Get An Answer': Ufos Catch Congress' Interest"*

we don't know who it is, and it's not ours. So we should know who it is, especially if it's an adversary that's made a technological leap."

But the situation appeared to be a stalemate. Without orders to deliver additional reports, the DOD went silent on the UAP issue once again, as if putting their heads in the sand would get Congress to go away.

The Pentagon's curtain of secrecy had been lifted for a moment... then, as always, the military had clamped down and refused to discuss the problem further. This time, public interest did not dissipate[13]. There was clearly a problem, some sort of inconsistency, and Congress refused to let the military off the hook this time[14].

UAPs had been brought into the mainstream—they were an undeniable reality, right there on paper, one that Congress could not ignore. A new chapter in the fight for UAP disclosure had begun.

AUGUST 2021: TAKING UP ARMS

Kirsten Gillibrand is not the kind of person you'd expect to be passionate about UAPs. A Democratic senator from New York with almost two decades of service, Gillibrand has consistently voted along party lines, and even considered a run for president in 2020. She's the very picture of a career politician.

And yet, when the first draft of the 2022 National Defense Act crossed her desk, Gillibrand did something very strange. She added an amendment to the Act that ordered the DOD to get serious about UAPs[15]. Alone among her peers, Gillibrand had taken a firm legislative stand on the issue. Other officials had been vocal about the dangers of ignoring the UAP report—but Gillibrand was the first to actually put her career on the line in search of answers.

Talking about unidentified objects has, for half a century, been political suicide. Yet somehow, Senator Gillibrand seems invulnerable to the usual stigma surrounding UAPs. Part of this invincibility results from her career history, her reliability. Marco Rubio (another UAP alarmist) had taken many questionable stances and flip-flopped through his career, but Gillibrand? Her record was solid. She was not prone to grandstanding, or Bernie-style blockading of others' goals. Unlike other Senators, she made few enemies during her time in public service, making her the perfect person to push for UAP disclosure.

But the fight wasn't over yet. As the deadline approached to pass the NDAA, Gillibrand found her new amendment under threat by the DOD.

Surprisingly, the Pentagon never asked Gillibrand to remove her amendment, or

---

13 *The Washington Post*, "How The Government Started Taking UFOs Seriously"

14 *Politico*, "'A Total Lack Of Focus': Lawmaker On A Mission To Compel Pentagon To Take UFOs Seriously"

15 *Congressional Record — Senate: November 4, 2021*

even to change it. Instead, they opted for guerilla warfare.

NOVEMBER 2021: "NOTHING TO SEE HERE, MOVE ALONG"

Proxy wars and psychological warfare are not new to the American military. And when pushed on the UAP issue, they defaulted to these tactics immediately.

To the DOD, the solution was simple: Why cave to Congress and be honest with the public, when they could simply set up their own UAP investigations office, and then bury the whole thing in red tape and bureaucracy? On November 23, 2021, that's exactly what they did. A surprise announcement by the Pentagon confirmed that, independent of Congressional orders, the Department of Defense had established a new office for investigating UAPs[16].

But something smelled rotten, and the civilian UAP community was quick to say so[17]. Likewise, ex-officials and members of Congress also expressed concern[18]. It seemed a tad convenient that only a month before the vote on the new National Defense Act—which just so happened to contain specific UAP-related legislation—the Pentagon had abruptly, out of nowhere, decided to care about UAPs, after 70 years of silence.

To those who had followed the DOD's history with UAPs, the move was sadly predictable. When confronted with evidence of strange craft in US skies, the Pentagon—and the CIA, for that matter[19]—have always stuck to their original, 1950's-era script. After the closing of Project Blue Book, the 1950s-era DOD investigation on UFOs, they made the choice to deny, obfuscate, and spread disinformation—and their approach in the 21st century was no different.

To start with, the DOD had chosen the clunkiest name imaginable for their new office. It was called "the Airborne Object Identification and Management Synchronization Group," which abbreviated to the monstrous acronym "AOIMSG." And if this weren't enough to dissuade the public's interest, they shoved this new office into a quiet, disused section of the Defense Department's vast bureaucracy.

The AOIMSG was placed under the Office of the Under Secretary of Defense for Intelligence & Security, also known as the OUSD(I&S). Now, like some kind of Lovecraftian alphabet soup, we had the AOIMSG, working for the OUSD(I&S), doing nebulously defined "research" on UAPs, formerly known as UFOs. Rolls right off the tongue, doesn't it?

---

16 US Department of Defense, "DoD Announces the Establishment of the Airborne Object Identification and Management Synchronization Group (AOIMSG)"

17 U.S. News, "New Pentagon Office Criticized as Effort to Control UFO Investigations, End Transparency"

18 The Hill, "Ex-Officials Voice Deep Concerns Over New Pentagon UFO Unit"

19 NSA Declassified Document - May-June 1981, "Is the CIA Stonewalling?"

BUREAUCRACY OF WEIRD

During the press conference announcing AOIMSG, there was audible laughter over the clunky abbreviation. Much more concerning, however, was the office's lack of investigative authority.

Under Gillibrand's legislation, the DOD would be required to chase every part of the UAP mystery, from the appearance of UAPs at nuclear sites[20] to the health effects of UAPs hovering near military personnel[21]. But the DOD's pale imitation of Gillibrand's office—the AOIMSG—would do none of these things[22]. It would, in effect, be a vestigial office of the government—a figurehead for the DOD to prop up without taking any real action.

Christopher Mellon once again expressed concern, writing in an open letter[23] that "as a former OSD staffer myself, I'm shocked that the DepSecDef would assign the UAP function to an oversight staff with no UAP funding, line authority, contracting, command or technical capabilities."

But Congress wasn't fooled. The NDAA went forward, its language unchanged, despite DOD pressure on officials to make adjustments to the text. And in December of 2021, the NDAA arrived on the floor of Congress, carrying the future of government UAP policy with it.

A Trojan horse of weirdness, cloaked in the comfortable banality of government paperwork, the Act stood poised to change everything about UAP research... or, if the DOD had their way, nothing whatsoever.

The final showdown had arrived.

DECEMBER 2021: FINISHING THE FIGHT

It has never been difficult to get funding for the American military. And it's only grown easier in the past few decades. In the years after 9/11, military spending exploded to a level never before seen in American history. In 2020, it was estimated that since 2001, America had spent a staggering $13.34 trillion dollars on defense[24], more than any other nation in the world. This mind-boggling amount of cash is even more astonishing, considering the fact that the Pentagon has never once passed a federal audit[25].

Every year, Americans fork over an astronomical amount on the military, and the military says "Don't worry, we spent it wisely. Just trust us." But in a curious twist of fate, this relentless spending with zero oversight is exactly what got Gillibrand's modified NDAA over the finish line. With a vote of 363 "ayes" to 70 "nays,"

20 The History Channel, "Why Have There Been So Many UFO Sightings Near Nuclear Facilities?"

21 Metro.co.uk, "Top-Secret Government Investigation 'Probed Health Effects Of Ufo Encounters'"

22 U.S. News, "New Pentagon Office Criticized as Effort to Control UFO Investigations, End Transparency"

23 Christopher Mellon, "Open Letter to Representative Gallego"

24 Scientific American, "It's Time to Rein in Inflated Military Budgets"

25 NPR, "The Pentagon Has Never Passed An Audit. Some Senators Want To Change That"

Congress easily passed the bill on December 7th, 2021[26] and President Biden signed it into law on December 27th[27]. While the public didn't know it, UAP researchers everywhere had just gotten a fantastic late Christmas gift—the Gillibrand UAP legislation was now law. The DOD was now legally required to pursue the UAP problem, and report yearly to Congress on the issue until at least 2026.

Was this the moment of truth? Had the "good guys" finally won? Can Fox Mulder hang up his gun and badge, satisfied The Truth will be pursued at last? Well... not exactly.

Since the passage of the NDAA, Congress and the DOD have continued to wrangle over its specifics, with the DOD dragging their feet on actually enacting any of the legislation[28]. And the Pentagon has ignored or deferred most press questions about the issue, showcasing their usual lack of tact, and a blunt refusal to address the problem with any honesty or integrity.

Despite Gillibrand's victory over her slippery foes in the military, the UAP question remains unresolved. Those of us in the UAP research community hope the new law will allow fresh data to be gathered, using the most powerful technology the military has to offer.

But some civilian groups have decided the DOD can't be trusted to deal honestly with the problem—and have decided to circumvent the military entirely.

In August of 2021, Harvard announced "Project Galileo," a civilian initiative to catalog and understand UAPs[29]. Putting aside the stigma usually associated with "flying saucers," this group will research and explore the UAP enigma, working with the public and civilian scientists instead of relying on secretive, classified military assets. In the aftermath of the NDAA, the race for the truth behind UAPs has split into two factions—civilian investigators like Project Galileo, and the military's NDAA-mandated, Congressionally funded investigation.

Who will be the first to establish an evidence-based theory of UAPs? Only time will tell. But as the situation develops and we learn more about our mysterious, disc-shaped visitors, *Planet Scumm* will keep you up-to-date on this strange, unfolding saga.

---

26   American Institute of Physics, "Congress Passes National Defense Authorization Act for Fiscal Year 2022"

27   The White House, "Statement by the President on S. 1605, the National Defense Authorization Act for Fiscal Year 2022"

28   US Department of Defense, "Pentagon Press Secretary John F. Kirby holds a Press Briefing"

29   The Crimson, "Harvard Prof. Loeb Launches 'Galileo Project,' Systematic Hunt for Signs of Extraterrestrial Life"

PLANETS/SCUMM

GAME OBJECTIVE

You are the amoeboid progeny of intergalactic deejay/menace, Scummy. Your "father" was blown to gooey bits by some two-bit bounty hunter— you and your siblings grew from the remains. Your mission? Take over the operation of Planet Scumm, a moon-sized broadcast ship bristling with weird creatures and tech. Do Scummy proud, and take revenge on the universe with style.

FOR THE PLAYERS

CREATE PSS (PLAYER-SCUMMS)

1. CHOOSE A <u>SCUMMSONA</u> (OR MAKE YOUR OWN [ADJECTIVE] + SCUMM):

» Spooky Scumm, Bubbly Scumm, Greasy Scumm, Lucky Scumm, Biggie Scumm, Nega-Scumm, Fancy Scumm, Wolfy Scumm

2. CHOOSE A <u>BROADCAST</u> FOR YOUR PS HOSTS:

» "Torture Tipz," "News and New Warrants," "Just A Full Two Hours of Static," "Doctors Without Boredom," "Unpopular Science," "Coup/Countercoup," or "Accretion Disco."

3. CHOOSE YOUR <u>NUMBER</u>, FROM 2 TO 5.

» A high number means you're better at PLANETS (macrotechnology; threats; over-the-top violence; impulsive, megalomaniacal action). A low number means you're better at SCUMM (biotechnology; charm and duplicity; literal sliminess; creepy, considered action).

4. CUSTOMIZE YOUR <u>CHARACTER</u>:

» Give your PS an endoplasm color and distinguishing accessory, like "red" and "mirrorshades," or "blue" and "mismatched galoshes."

PLAYER GOAL:

» For example, portray a pulpy space villain that knows how to party. Hard.

CHARACTER GOAL—CHOOSE ONE OR CREATE YOUR OWN:

» Become the head deejay and new Scummy

» Bring Planet Scumm's broadcasts to a new market

» Destroy Earth

» Clear out Scummy's garage

» Produce offspring via budding

» Meet a new alien species

» Bring Scummy back to life

» Host the galaxy's biggest party.

ASSETS AND LIABILITIES

Planet Scumm is too big and poorly maintained to accurately map. However, your initial explorations have revealed a few useful things, plus a few... troubling things.

AS A GROUP, PICK THREE ASSETS FOR THE NEW BROADCAST CREW:

» Planet-killer laser, Unused Scummy voice recordings, Cloning bay, Overclocked secondary engines, Miniature human society that worships Scummy, Always-stocked minibar, Military uniforms for most space-faring civilizations, Single-use time machine

THEN, PICK TWO LIABILITIES:

» Sizable intern rebellion, Ship-mite infestation, Mirror Universe Scummy (with goatee), Big hole getting bigger, Missing record collection, Low fuel reserves, Declining ratings, Unlocked clown pens.

YOU HAVE:

» Technology and resources appropriate for a science-fiction laboratory and a pirate radio station.

ROLLING THE DICE

WHEN YOU DO SOMETHING RISKY

» Roll **1D6** to find out how it goes.

» Roll **+1D** if you're **PREPARED**, and **+1D** if you're an **EXPERT**.

» If you're using **PLANETS**, you want to roll *under* your number.

» If you're using **SCUMM**, you want to roll over your number.

IF NONE OF YOUR DICE SUCCEED

» It goes wrong. The GM says how things get worse for you.

IF ONE DIE SUCCEEDS

» You do it, but it's messy. The GM inflicts a complication, harm, or cost.

IF TWO DICE SUCCEED

» You *Just Do It*. Hooray!

IF THREE DICE SUCCEED

» You get a critical success. The GM describes an extra effect you achieve.

IF YOU ROLL YOUR NUMBER EXACTLY

» You sync your mind's eye with **CONSTELLATION SCUMM**. No matter where you are, Planet Scumm arrives (or otherwise reaches out) and does something on top of whatever you rolled for. You tell the GM what Planet Scumm does in that moment.

HELPING

» If you want to help someone who's rolling, describe what your PS does, and make a roll yourself. If you succeed, give them **+1D**.

FOR THE GAMEMASTER

Play to find out how the PSs screw everything up. Introduce the threat by showing how it interferes (even tangentially) with the *Planet Scumm* broadcast. Before the threat does something, make it clear what's about to happen, then ask the players what they want to do.

Call for a roll when the outcome of an action is uncertain. Don't pre-plan anything—let the slime flow where it may. Use failure and screwy action to push the story forward. For good, ill, or odd, the situation should *always* change after a roll.

GM: CREATE A DELICATE SITUATION (FOR THE PSs TO RUIN)

» Roll on the tables below for instant story structure.

SOME JERKS...

1	Transdimensional Oligarchs	**4**	Cyborg Bees
2	The Clown Nebula	**5**	Space Fascists Consciously Imitating the Galactic Empire from "Star Wars"
3	Lotar Slime-Killer and Friends	**6**	Foolish Earthlings

WANT TO...

1	Destroy	**4**	Outlaw
2	Steal	**5**	Copy
3	Control	**6**	Blockade

THE...

1	*Planet Scumm* broadcast	**4**	Space-time continuum
2	Last remaining Disco Sun	**5**	Scummy's last will & testament
3	Foolish planet, Earth	**6**	Not the Death Star, but definitely a death star

THE TWIST?

1	It was a dream the whole time!	4	Grandfather paradox!
2	Secret robots!	5	Experiment arranged by aliens!
3	Sudden yet inevitable betrayal!	6	It's a cookbook! *A COOKBOOK!*

CREDITS

» *"Planets/Scumm" is a hack of "Lasers & Feelings" by One Seven Design, adapted by Planet Scumm Editor-in-Chief and RPG architect, Sean Clancy.*

MEET THE SLIMELING

What's a Slimeling? Why, with a little effort (and a monthly contribution of $3) ANYONE can become a slimeling—which power our proprietary squid-based word processing solution, "Squidner." If you can think of an easier way to source ink, *we'd like to see it.* (Honestly, we would.)

SIGN UP FOR OUR $3 "SLIMELING" TIER ON PATREON AND YOU'LL ENJOY:

» A digital book subscription. Get each new ebook on the day of release.

» Early access to "Planet Scumm" music and audio projects.

» Access to exclusive postcards, stickers, and/or art prints.

» $5 off at the "Planet Scumm" store

» Invitation to our Author / Artist Discord

» Other Scummy swag rocketing your way on a semi-regular basis.

Plus, you'll be able to take pride in the fact that you're helping to keep independent publishing chugging right along here on planet Earth.

ONCE MORE FOR EMPHASIS—
VISIT PATREON.COM/PLANETSCUMM FOR ALL YOUR SCI-FI AND SLIME-BUY NEEDS.

And when you're done there, take a look in the mirror. 'Cause that slimeling you just met? *They're you*